D1795163

MiSTRESS
OF THE
ROCK

Copyright © 2007 by Myron Edwards.

ISBN: Hardcover   978 – 1 –945286 – 17 – 9
        Softcover   978 – 1 – 945286 – 14 - 8
        Ebooks   978 – 1 – 945286 – 15 – 5
                     978 – 1 – 945286 – 16 - 2

All rights reserved. No part of this book may be reproduced or transmitted in any form or by any means, electronic or mechanical, including photocopying, recording, or by any information storage and retrieval system, without permission in writing from the copyright owner.

This is a work of fiction. Names, characters, places and incidents either are the product of the author's imagination or are used fictitiously, and any resemblance to any actual persons, living or dead, events, or locales is entirely coincidental.

Revised 5/31/2017

RockHill Publishing LLC
PO Box 62241
Virginia Beach, VA
23466-2241

www.rockhillpublishing.com

MISTRESS
OF THE
ROCK

BY MYRON EDWARDS

Table of Contents

BELIEVE

This book is dedicated to my children.

'Dream your dreams and believe in them, for one day they will come true.'

This book would not have been possible without the following people to whom my debt can never be repaid.

My wife Niki and my good friends – Mat, Val, Helen, Mark, Denny, Darren, Christen
Mike, Max, Tina, Maria, David, Phil and to all those who gave me the inspiration to keep going.

Special thanks to Lili Panagi of Pan Media who never doubted me.

And to James Hill and Athina Paris for their support, energy, and faith.

Myron Edwards

CHAPTER ONE

CYPRUS 1991

'Corporal Richard Cole reporting, Sir.'

'You're late, Cole. Get on board now, the transport leaves in twenty minutes.'

'Yes, Sir.'

Cole's kit was already heavy and the extra burden of running for the plane left him breathless. He thought he was fit at twenty-five, and he should have been, but apparently, he still needed extra exercise. He bolted up the steps and boarded the transport plane, taking the seat next to a young soldier who was far too wrapped up in a magazine to notice him.

Richard removed his cap, revealing a short haircut for the trip, as deserts were not the place for hair that touched shirt collars. In the intense heat, he stroked the back of his head. His hands returned wet and his face dripped droplets of sweat, which fell onto his fatigues. He looked around as he leaned back on the rough seat. He was about the same size as most of the other soldiers but his youthful looks made him look younger than his age purported and that of his companions. His face also appeared well-tanned compared to the pasty expressions of some of his fellow travellers. And like Richard, all were in uniform and kitted up to their eyeballs. Everyone buckled in and waited for take-off.

1

It was February thirteenth. The Gulf War, Part One, had begun just over a month ago and the air-war was in full swing. The despot Saddam had been as stubborn and ruthless as the day he invaded Kuwait in the summer of 1990. The diplomacy that followed by various countries and the UN was going nowhere, so the order to initiate an airstrike came on January sixteen. The ground war would soon follow. It was where the aircraft was headed.

War had never occurred to Richard when he first signed up. Sure, the Falklands had stirred the patriotism of the British people and made the country proud again but although the Falklands was a bitter and bloody conflict it was a domestic affair between two countries, Argentina and Britain, and if most 'Brits' were honest at the time, not many of them knew where the fucking Falklands were anyway. It was, after all, Maggie Thatcher's Waterloo and it worked for her.

This Gulf War had much wider and sinister connotations. Not only were the 'Brits' involved but also most of the free world, with the US fronting the adventure. For whatever reason was given, there was no doubting Saddam was dangerous for the world, with the implications for the Middle East frightening. Under this cloud of uncertainty and fear, the green and pleasant land of England would seem a million miles away, even though they were only just a few hours from the hot scorching desert of Kuwait.

En-route to Kuwait they stopped in Cyprus, landing at the civilian airport in Paphos, as the military fields of Akrotiri and Dhekalia were already full to overflowing with combat aircraft of all types and sizes.

At Paphos, the plane touched down around 4pm, the sun still hot as the troops left the aircraft and thumped down the metal stairs to the awaiting trucks, boarding twenty men at a time. Richard took the last place at the back of his truck. The engine roared with life and with all formalities of customs and immigration dispensed with, it began to rumble along the coastal road out of Paphos. After all, this was war, albeit secretly hosted on Cyprus.

This was Richard's first visit to the island and from what he could see from the back of the truck it looked like a fine place to visit. From his small vantage point at the back, there seemed to be a good deal of activity going on, with lots of cars and people hurrying about. And amongst them was a collection of Greek Cypriot soldiers kitted out in green camouflage uniforms waiting along the roadside.

In this tourist-like atmosphere it was all too easy to forget that this was a divided land, invaded by the Turks in 1974, after an unsuccessful coup by the Greeks led by then-President and Archbishop Makarios. The island was divided by a thin green line which ran from the North to the South and was policed by the UN. Under such circumstances the fragile peace inevitably seemed vulnerable, yet it held.

The green line was a constant reminder to the Cypriot people in the south that their island was occupied—at least some of it including the wonderful beach resorts of Kyrenia and Famagusta, which were cut off and entrenched with mine fields and guarded by Turks.

These resorts had once been deemed to be among the classiest in the Mediterranean, with hotels and restaurants patronised by tourists from the world over. Only now, these fine accommodations and eateries were home to the rats, snakes and scorpions that occupied them. The analogy of vermin in these occupied resorts was a good description of the occupiers for many Greeks. Still, it remained a sad and sorry state of affairs that those who were about to become involved in a new conflict could not resolve this one first. Perhaps one day they would try.

As the truck started to move out of town, the convoy meandered along the picturesque road towards the base at Episkopi. The sun had begun to dim and the road became windier, as the trucks struggled round and around the bends, slowly at first then accelerating through the gears to gain momentum. The driver purposely crunching the gears from time to time just to make sure none of his occupants had fallen asleep. The inside of the truck was hot, the new temperature something the soldiers were not yet acclimatised to. As the convoy reached a tight bend, one of the guys at the front looked out of the canvas window and shouted to the rest of his companions. 'That's Aphrodite's Rock.'

Richard looked out of the back of the open truck and saw one large rock embedded in the shore and two smaller ones rooted in the sea. The sun reflected on their colour, making them shimmer against the stunning blues of the Mediterranean. The white tufts of surf lapping against the base of the rocks as if licking them.

'Petra Tou Romiou the Greeks call it, birthplace of Aphrodite. Goddess of LOVE,' purposely accentuated to make an impact.

'What, those old rocks?' came Richard's somewhat bemused retort.

'Yep, that was where she was born, they say, came out of the sea, just there.'

'Bollocks.' Richard's astute friend of the magazine made his contribution.

'Precisely, that is what she's made of, some Greek god's bollocks, well, dick actually, cut off and thrown into the sea from which came Aphrodite. *Aphro,* meaning from the foam.'

'You're a scholar then?' Richard asked his learned friend at the front.

'No, just read it in the guide book. Amazing what you can learn from these things.' He passed the book down to the back of the truck.

Richard opened it to the page on Aphrodite's Rock, nodding his thanks.

Magazine man raised his head. 'Must be an omen, seeing that today, what with it being Valentine's tomorrow, maybe we'll get a shag.' The last comment was lost in the laughter that now enveloped the rest of the truck as the convoy wound its way higher up the hill and over the escarpment of Aphrodite's Rock, which had finally slipped out of sight.

As the trucks entered the gates at Episkopi they had their first good view of what the place was like and on seeing it, it felt as if they had never left England, for Episkopi appeared just like England in every detail. True, the Cypriots drove their cars on the same side of the road as in England, but this wasn't just about driving. All the houses, the signs and the notices were as if they were still in Aldershot—brick-built quarters and barracks, road signs in English, with little or no concessions to the Greek language. There was even a café that served all-day English breakfast.

Around the base were a few Cypriots but most of them wore some form of uniform or another, be it cleaner or military. Richard hoped there would be time to look around before the harsh reality of war cut into his tour of the emplacements and the night life.

Valentine's Day brought home the true reality of the War. In Baghdad, a coalition air raid had hit a civilian bunker, killing 314 men, women, and children. This was the true cost of war but why should it be waged on the innocent? Richard mused over the report.

The next few days involved training and retraining with weapons and chemical apparatus, as the threat of a chemical attack was very real. But in the quiet corridors of politics there seemed just a glimmer of hope that they might not have to fight. Tariq Aziz, the Iraqi Deputy Minister had flown to Moscow to try and stop further conflict by negotiating with the Russians.

No luck.

By the 21st of February all practices were over and the troops were ready, gear stowed and stacked on board with helicopters eager to fly into the fury. There were already covert ops going on in the desert on a need-to-know basis and which, most of those in the camp, didn't need or want to know. Those commandos kept themselves to themselves, and never contacted other divisions, unless they had to.

The daily training had toned and honed muscles and Richard was now fighting fit, at least physically. His mental state however needed further training. The waiting was playing on everybody's nerves, but this game belonged solely to the politicians. The suspicions emanating around the camp were that soon it would begin for Richard and all those with him. The next day, February 22nd, President Bush ordered the withdrawal of enemy forces from Kuwait. It didn't happen, and Richard was on his way.

Disciplined energetic soldiers gathered on the parade ground en-route to whatever fate lay in store for them. Orders given, the assembled troops swiftly moved to the waiting helicopters. The Chinook Copters rose slowly into the air, then banked turning out towards the sea. Silence ran through the crowded aircraft. Only the chug-chug engine sounds and the whirling blades could be heard as they whisked through the air with force and velocity. The night began to creep in and the horizon faded to a black stillness as the helicopters slipped out to sea hugging the coastline. In the distance, Richard caught a glimpse of Aphrodite's Rock, which he had seen just over a week ago. The moon that had now settled, cast a beam that beckoned to him and he thought of this as a homing signal. Could the Goddess be telling him that she would bring him back safely? In silent prayer, he urged her that she would. But would she hear him?

CHAPTER TWO

KUWAIT

At night, the desert was cold, bitterly cold and the wind blew hard against the skin and by day it scorched the earth under the feet. However, the movement of uniformed people of all shapes and sizes was amazing to see. Everyone seemed to know where they were going through the organised chaos of pre-battle.

Missile alerts were fairly frequent but nothing actually happened. There was almost always a collective 'Thank God' expression that echoed throughout the camp after every false alarm. But all of them knew that one day, one hour, or one minute, one of those attacks would be for real.

Iraq had already attacked Israel with Scud missiles earlier in January. Though somewhat slow and cumbersome, those weapons had the desired effect as they signalled Saddam's pre-publicised threat to launch an attack. The world had waited for Israel's response, knowing their capability would be either conventional or something more. The Israelis', metaphorically and militarily speaking, kept their hands in their pockets, leaving the fighting to someone else.

During the waiting, Richard had become accustomed to the bravado and innuendo of the combatants. He was after all in the Army, not a bowling team. The subjects that permeated most of the conversations were sex, politics and religion, much of which could be summed up in one simple phrase. 'God help us! I hope the fucking President knows what he's doing!'

Letters home was the other main occupation for many of the soldiers. In snatched moments, a few urgent words were scrawled down on pre-prepared cards or paper with just a hint of the emotions that were running through the writer. For those who had eloquence of phrase with more than GCSE English O Level, the sentiment was clear. But for those whose command of the written word was more oblique, then it was left to the reader to form their own opinion of what emotions were being exchanged. Richard found himself somewhere in the middle, as his wife, son, and baby daughter occupied all of his words as he wrote.

Hello Julie, darling,

I wish I could tell you what I am doing here. I didn't sign up for this, but I suppose it's a soldier's lot and duty to go where he is sent. I can tell you this, it's not a very hospitable place and a lot is going on. I find it difficult to put into words exactly what it is I want to say as I have never been faced with anything like this before and it's not easy to think that by the time you receive this I might not be here anymore. I realise this is not what you expect to read but who knows what might happen? Sorry for sounding so bleak. I have made arrangements should anything happen but I am confident it won't. We are all geared up and ready to go, so hopefully it will be over soon. I am sure you will follow it all on TV. That sounds odd, doesn't it, watching war on the television as it happens. I pray that I get through this. Please

*cuddle the kids for me and make sure they know that I miss
and love them very much, as I miss and love you.*
Always, for a day and evermore,
Richard

He folded the letter, put it into an envelope, and left it on
the table for collection. The scream of the siren heralded a
new attack so he ran for cover as fast as he could.

The next few hours saw the activity rise considerably, the
imminent attack grew closer and closer, the pressure point
was about to be reached. Richard lay on his canvas bed
hidden in the pages of his guidebook. He had already read it
almost from cover to cover and probably knew as much
about Cyprus and the Aphrodite legend as the local tourist
guide, but somehow, he wanted to learn more. But now was
clearly not the time to do it. If he came through this he would
try to get closer to the mystery of Aphrodite's Rock, because
he was sure there was a mystery behind it. It simply needed
someone to uncover it. Those three rocks in the sand
couldn't be all there was to the legend. There had to
be something more, but what? Wrapping himself up in
history and myth brought him comfort from the fear that lay
ahead. Perhaps it was this more than anything else that he
asked for when he had prayed to the Goddess in the
helicopter. Yes, he wanted safe passage and to get home, but
above all, he wanted something to take his mind off the terror
that he felt inside. In an odd kind of way, she was already
providing it.

The morning of the 24th of February started like most
mornings, with the desert sun rising early and cutting its rays
across the orange coloured sands. As the last remnants of a
lazy moon disappeared out of the sky, the sun burnt bright

and shadows became long and low as if in their design they painted the ground.

Across the makeshift parade ground, soldiers and combatants of all ranks and denominations made their way from one place to the next. Exercise was in full swing, as discipline or recreation and the buzz of anticipation was all around the camp.

Richard stood by his tent watching then looked across to the approaching figure and seemed to recognise him, but from where he was not sure.

'Good morning,' the stranger spoke with authority in his voice, and across his uniform he displayed several winged badges. He was not as tall as Richard but was broader in shape, if not muscular, well-built, solid, his face well-tanned and his eyes blue. His hair was a dark brown, bordering on black with just the hint of a few strands of grey peeping through. Undoubtedly, among his most redeeming features was his smile, which was broad and wide and genuine.

Richard gauged his age at about thirty to thirty-five.

'Peter Shaw, I was your pilot, on the bird that brought you over.'

Richard looked somewhat bemused. 'Bird...'

'The copter, mate, I brought you out here. Peter Shaw, pilot.' Peter repeated himself. 'Good to see you!'

'Yes, great, thanks. Sorry, the bird,'

'Oh shit, don't mind me, bird, choppers, copters, all the same. So, how are you getting on, settling in? These drills are a real pain, aren't they?'

Richard starts to remember the journey over and his prayer to the goddess. It brings a wide grin to his face. 'Richard, Richard Cole.' He too repeated himself as if to make sure Peter knew whom he was talking to. 'Good to meet you too!'

Peter carried on with his conversation as if he had not heard Richard's intro. 'All necessary I guess. Hate to think those Iraqis would use the stuff, but can't be too careful. They have done it before.'

The Siren sounded on cue and the two scattered towards the makeshift shelter.

Peter just has time for one last expression before ducking down into the shelter. 'FUCK, here we go again!'

'It seems so!' Richard's nod confirmed the situation.

The all clear sounded and the anxious soldiers and troops exited from their shelters, another drill it would seem over.

Later that morning, Peter returned to Richard. As both stood outside the tent chatting, Peter puffed on a small cheroot-style cigar with his expression one of melancholy. 'Bastards killed twenty-eight Yanks today, and over a hundred injured. Some bastard missile it was, in Saudi.'

'They're bombing cities now, before we ever get near the battlefield. What do you think they're going to do next?'

'Not sure. Us probably! They have already had a go at Israel, remember, so anything's possible!'

'Have you heard anything about when it might start?'

'Just rumours. They say not long now.' Peter drags on the cigar and a puff of grey smoke exits from his mouth.

'I will just be glad to go. I hate waiting around, all that adrenalin pumped up and nowhere to go.' Richard turned towards his new friend. 'You ever think you might not come back from one of these flights of yours?'

'Sometimes, yeah, but then I think if it's going to happen there's fuck all I can do about it! Besides, I like flying. Might do it when I get out, that's if someone will have me. Only another year to go, then I am out.'

'Four for me, just don't know what I'll do when I get out though. Got a trade here as an electrician, but I think I'd like to do something else. I might get into computers. That's the future, so they say. Anyway, I just think I would like to try something different.'

'Well, I hope it all works out for you. Got any kids?'

'Two little ones, Matthew and Molly. There's just a year between them, Matthew's two and Molly is my baby. You?'

'Not yet, said we'll try when I get back. Sheila, my Missus wanted to get the house and stuff sorted first. I said she got it arse backwards but would she listen? NO! Still, she is the one who has to carry the little buggers, not me. I just have to make sure the swimmers get in the pool.'

'Well, that's the fun bit, Peter.'

'You can say that again. Anyway, Rich, I am out of here. Catch up with you later.'

The two smiled and chuckled together and for an instant, the war was forgotten, then, Peter walked away.

Richard turned and went back inside. Sitting on his bunk-bed, he grabbed the book about the rock, sat down and began to read it again. He picked up another book and placed it beside the other one. Greek Myths was the title. He had found this one in the make-shift library set up on the camp.

As day turned to night, large groups of troops moved across the desert supported by a plethora of aircraft, tanks, trucks, missile bombardments, and artillery fire. The night sky lit up for miles around.

Richard, in contrast, regularly sat in his tent almost oblivious to the noise and the movement; but finally, his curiosity kicked in and he got up to look out of the tent-flap to observe all the activity, patiently waiting for his turn to be called. Then he returned to his bed and started re-reading the books.

Private Jones entered the tent kitted out for war. He was younger than Richard and not too smart; some would call him a grunt in certain circles, but that would be a little harsh on him. But there was no doubting the excitement in his face. If anything, you could see Jones' adrenalin flowing through his veins as he pointed to the action unfolding in front of them. 'Hey Corp, come and see this, it's like a fucking armada out there, if that's what you call it.' Jones pointed and left just as quickly as he had entered.

Richard looked out of his tent and then skywards. Red flashing lights dotted the black sky and the noise of engines pierced the desert silence. He turned back to his bed and sat down to read, again waiting for the call. Then he spoke aloud, as if to drown out the chaos around him, looking for a sanctuary, which he always found in the pages of the books. 'I have to go back to Cyprus, I know Julie will love it, and I'm sure she'll feel the same way as I do. I just know it. Just as I know there is something more to this goddess thing, but what?'

The terror they all felt was about to be unleashed, with the President's order to begin the ground war. Under cover of a desert night, the troops began to advance, equipped with night vision and machines that sported technical wizardry, designed to baffle and batter the maligned Iraqi army, most of whom were frightened and undisciplined conscripts skulking in their fox holes.

But in the space of just twenty-four hours since the assault, it was effectively all over, President Bush announced to a grateful nation that the troops had liberated Kuwait City. The force of the coalition had frightened resistance out of the Iraqis. The threatened chemical or gas attacks never came and the whole ground war was over in forty-eight hours. Saddam's last desperate act was to set the oil wells on fire, believing that crippling the west's oil reserves would be something of a victory, even if a shallow one.

Peter was in a jubilant mood as he entered Richard's tent. Without thought and unable to contain his excitement, he plopped down hard onto the bed, waking Richard instantly. 'Rich, quick, come see this!'

Richard, still sleepy and bemused followed Peter outside.

A large TV screen had been set up and was broadcasting to the troops who had gathered around it. A ticker news tape displayed at the bottom of the screen proclaimed news of the victory, supported by pictures of Kuwaiti residents waving US flags as they welcomed troops, the images further reinforced by the noise of several hundred cheering voices.

'It's all over mate, and you missed it!'

'What? What do you mean missed it?' Richard rubbed his eyes to clear the night before and to look on a new day.

'THE WAR, it's over, they're in Kuwait, we just have to mop up and then we can fuck off back home.'

'You're joking, aren't you? It can't be over.'

Peter began grinning wildly, slapping Richard on the back. 'Look at the screen, it is over. Well, almost. Just need the Iraqis to surrender officially, then that's it. They just chucked in the towel and they've gone. There's no one left to fight.'

'NO, no, it can't be. And I slept through it?' Richard's realisation finally sunk in.

'SHIT, so what! Just be glad it's over and there's not a scratch on any of us.'

'Yeah, you're right!' Richard watched as the soldiers celebrated and small clusters of men and women rejoiced together. Privates' Jones, Edwards, Thomas and Banks, and a couple of the other men Richard didn't know walked over towards Peter and Richard and began shaking hands, smiling brightly, a look that decorated all their faces, as a sense of relief spread through the camp. Richard joked and listened and chatted with the others, and kept thinking how lucky he was. He had prepared himself for battle, had trained himself to battle readiness, and had also made his peace with God. Now, he almost felt cheated, exhilarated that he was alive and unscathed, yet, not tested. It was, as it was described to him later, two mismatched boxers in a ring, one flailing away to get in a punch, whilst the other pummelled the other into submission. The bout was over in just four rounds, or four days in war speak.

The following day, Iraq accepted all UN resolutions and everybody began to pack up to go home.

With the threat of any attack diminished, the camp relaxed and over the next two days, the atmosphere was almost cordial. Just outside the main camp area, Richard and Peter had found a quiet place to have a drink, a kind of farewell drink, as soon, they would be splitting up, going their separate ways, and back to their units. They lay down on the desert sand, between them a second bottle of sparkling vino they had started and was almost gone. It too would soon find a spot next to the empty bottle that already lay beside them.

Peter brushed off the sand with his hands and stood up, a little unsteady at first but quickly corrected himself. 'Well, I'd better get back to the unit. Maybe we will catch up later.'

'I hope so. Thanks.' Richard raised the now just about empty bottle to Peter as a gesture of farewell. Almost as an afterthought he too stood up and took Peter's hand. 'Peter, you've been a good mate to have around.'

'No problems. I hope we can stay friends! After all this has passed us by. Anyway, better go, or I will get bollocked, for being AWOL. Good luck.' Peter said and began to walk away.

Richard called him back with his next statement, just as Peter moved forward and took a final swig from the bottle.

'Do you feel cheated, Pete?'

'Cheated, why?'

'We trained all those years to get ready to fight and to prove ourselves and now we don't have to. All those exercises, the effort, adrenalin, and fear locked up inside. That's what I mean by cheated.'

Peter placed his hand on his friend's shoulder. 'No, Rich, I don't feel cheated. I just feel glad to be alive and out of it, and so should you.'

'I do too, Pete. I feel glad to be alive. But I can't help thinking that I've missed something, something that I should have done or seen, something important.'

'No, you haven't, you've just been lucky. We all have, really! So, I'm grateful for that…Good luck and see you around.' Peter shook Richards's hand, they hugged once more then both went their separate ways.

CHAPTER THREE

HIGHWAY 80

Richard felt content as he slumbered under his single sheet, his rest only interrupted by the face of his Sergeant cowering down upon him.

'COLE! COLE! Get up! We are needed somewhere.'

Richard responded to the summons immediately and within a minute or two of his wakening was up, dressed, and ready for the day. 'I am packed, Sergeant, all set for the off.'

'Not today, Cole, you are going with me. We have an observation to carry out. Get your gear and be ready outside, in five.'

'Yes, Sergeant,' Richard said as he looked around the tent and shuffled a few items into his kit bag.

Sergeant Hancock was a soldier's soldier, who had been around some time and had seen action in places that most people would shudder at the thought of, including Northern Ireland and the Falklands. His experience was invaluable in a tight spot and he was as strict as he was compassionate. Kuwait would be his final duty, as he was set to leave the army as soon as they got home.

The blades of the helicopter were already spinning and the dust being thrown up made Cole cover his face immediately. Hancock bundled him into the chopper, and

Richard looked towards the front, Peter was not the pilot. The craft ascended slowly at first then faster as the ground moved further away from them. Richard could hear the sound of the rotors and that was about all he could hear as they pulled away from base camp and out into the desert.

'We are going to pick up a jeep, from there we are going across the desert to these coordinates,' Hancock pointed down to a map he held in his hand. 'There is some big party going on with the Yanks and they just want us to observe, ok?'

Richard nodded his understanding of the situation.

The copter began to descend. They couldn't have been in the air more than fifteen minutes but the scarred landscape below bore testimony to a war that was in its last throes. The crumpled machinery lay burning, as plumes of black smoke rose into the clouds.

Both men jumped from the copter and began running towards the barely visible camouflaged jeep, parked close to a sand dune. Wasting no time, Hancock pulled off the camouflage and jumped in, Richard looked back towards the chopper, which was already in the air, as he stepped into the jeep.

Sergeant Hancock was in the driver's seat revving the engine, waiting on Cole. Richard clambered in beside him and the jeep sped off, the trail of dust and spinning tires leaving a tale in the sand.

Hancock said nothing as he kept driving and looking down at the map. Richard too said nothing and looked ahead. There was nothing visible, just sand, sand, and more sand heaped into dunes or furrowed out into small holes. But the further they distanced themselves from camp, more remnants of an army in retreat lay scattered across the ground and as they approached the Kuwaiti border, two other jeeps joined them. They acknowledged each other and in a threesome headed towards the border.

For the first time since they left, Hancock turned to Cole and above the roar and thumping of the engine and the road noise below them told him what was happening. 'The Republican Guard are trying to get out of Kuwait, making a run for it, and taking whatever they can with them. As I said, the Yanks are looking to give them a farewell party, going to bust them open. It's our job to watch and listen. We only engage them if we have to, understood?'

'Yes, Sergeant,' whatever way this turned out it would be Cole's first action.

The jeep bumped and thumped and trundled from gear to gear over the terrain. Cole and Hancock were more than once bounced and thrown up and down in their seats before reaching their destination, the Jeep slowing down, before stopping on a small incline.

In the distance, was the fast approaching sight of billowing pillars of black smoke edging up towards the sun. Encamped in their observation spot, the two men watched as the bombs and precision rockets homed in on their targets. Sporadic and then more controlled gunfire spurted out across the landscape as faint screams and more gunfire echoed across the dirty road in front of them.

Richard looked up, the scream of jets above and the silence of the smoke rising provided a surreal backdrop to the carnage unfolding below them. He gripped the chinstrap of his helmet and tightened it as he lay down closer to the top of the incline for a better view away from harm's way, his heavyweight field binoculars already focused on the landscape ahead. He could see the signpost Highway 80 written in Arabic as well as English, the road markings with the figure 80 just visible.

It was 8:00am and already the blazing sun added to the intense discomfort of their surroundings. Slowly, Cole and the Sergeant edged closer to the highway and began to witness the battle as the other two jeeps headed east, away from the highway.

At first it was difficult to make out what was happening, as the highway was littered with a convoy of military and commercial vehicles, tanks, personnel carriers, army lorries, buses, cars, and vans. Everything seemed to be aflame. Among the wreckage of exploding vehicles were scores of bodies. Some were dead soldiers still in their uniforms. Others were civilians, men, women, and children, all clustered together in a vain attempt to escape and all lying on the ground in small huddled groups. Inside one of the buses, some children were still in their seats on the bullet splattered bus, their bloodied faces turned against the remains of the glass windows.

Richard eased his body closer to the road. He was sure he could be seen now, as more waves of airstrikes continued to pound the road. Amongst the weapons used were deadly heat-seeking missiles which snaked their way through the air and the wreckage, before smacking into their targets and spreading more carnage and mayhem as well as dense palls of smoke that rose into tall pillars. Cries of agony accompanied each strike, followed by a silence which seemed to absorb and eat up the impact. Engines raced and throbbed as more vehicles tried to run the gauntlet, only to be hemmed in by constant machine gun and rifle fire.

Some of the firing came from inside the twisted metal of the wrecked cars, as desperate insurgence fired back in retaliation; the occupants trying to shoot at the helicopters, tanks or halftracks closing in on them. For a few brief seconds, it was their guns blazing in retaliation, the familiar rattle of their AK 47's in full voice only to be silenced by a direct hit on their vehicle, which rapidly became engulfed by flames, in the entrapped convoy.

Throughout, Richard watched and listened and now a new sense kicked in, that of smell. The smoke smelt acrid and tasted bitter and he began to cough and choke on the fumes, but it was not just the smoke that drew the bile to Richard's throat and mouth. It was the stench of burning flesh and spilled fuel, mixed with the raw metallic smell of bullets crashing on metal before they ricocheted into innocents, which left the area caked in a phosphorous aroma drifting across them, as more blood spilled into puddles before them. Richard drew his binoculars back from his eyes as the sweat dribbled from his forehead.

Hancock looked at him and began to laugh, enough to crack a dent in the serenade of combat.

'What?' Richard's bemused expression added even more curiosity to the reason he was laughing and such levity in such a desolate situation.

'Cole, I wish I had a mirror, or better still a camera. You should see yourself. You look like a fucking Panda.'

'What?' The same word repeated as Richard stared into the lens of the binoculars reflecting his somewhat unusual look. The rings of the binoculars had mingled with his sweat and two black rings now rimmed his eyes. He reached for a cloth handkerchief and wiped away the rings.

'Here, take this.' Hancock handed Richard a small jar of Vaseline. 'Make sure you put plenty under your nose.'

Richard took the jar, opened it, and promptly placed a large dollop of the gel under his nose and along his face. He handed the jar back to Hancock who repeated the action.

'We need to move in closer. Keep sharp and if you see something that needs killing, kill it.'

Richard breathed deep. The Vaseline was working. It was all he could smell as they both slithered down the hill to another observation point to take up their positions. This one, less than two-hundred yards from the highway.

A small troop of American soldiers led by their Corporal walked gingerly towards the colony. The soldiers were all heavily armed; some with M16's took cover behind some of the smouldering wrecks as they picked their way through the remains to find better targets.

Hancock crept nearer, moving across the ground on his belly, before nodding to Richard to stay close and pointing to a spot even closer to the roadway. Cole edged himself along the ground, he too crawling towards the place. It was a burnt-out lorry, one of the first hit, as it cooked in the sun. Cole lay below the chassis, to watch as the Corporal signalled to his troops to head down the road.

The troops fired into vehicles, looking for anyone with a gun or a bomb. They continued to search and *reckie* in single file and then in twos along the column, moving from one vehicle to the next, mopping up any stragglers, regardless of their look.

A single shot rang out against the metal shell of a truck close to where the Corporal stood. His troops returned fire in a volley of rounds and rallied around the wreckage of a bus.

In the distance, more troops could be seen running towards the group. Hand grenades were tossed into vehicles almost casually, and exploded, as more civilians hiding in the vehicles died mercilessly.

The mopping up operation of the convoy continued without hesitation as the jets screeched high above them and the helicopters hovered and sprayed the road with machine-gun fire from inside, cutting off any possible retreat. Explosions ripped through the highway as pockets of the road opened with great gaping holes, bright orange coloured flames shot out from them, stretching skyward.

Richard watched, not moving a muscle, as the troops continued to clean the area.

From behind a wrecked car, an Arab woman emerged, clutching a bundle in her arms. It looked like a baby wrapped in a single blanket. The woman wore a long black one-piece dress, her face was covered by a black veil, just her eyes showing through a gap in the material, and her dress was ripped and splattered with blood and dirt as she staggered out from her hiding place towards the soldiers. Richard focused his binoculars on her. There was no sound as he watched her stumble forward on her way to the troops who stood with their guns aimed at her.

Once more, she fell to her knees; her arms outstretched, pleading for someone to take the bundle from her. She slipped again and Richard could clearly see that one side of her body was covered in thick blood oozing out of a deep wound, flowing freely, spattering the ground under her.

The Corporal moved closer flanked by his troops but cautious of any possible suicide bomber, he stood two to three feet from her. She stretched out her hands and arms and offered the bundle to him again. Reaching forward, she unclipped the veil from her face. It was an act of total surprise for the Corporal, something he never had seen before—an Arab woman unveiling herself to an infidel. He deemed the gesture an act of honesty as the woman smiled, revealing her young face with its light skin and piercing dark eyes that opened wider as she watched him take the bundle from her.

A smile spread across her face. It was her last emotion, for once she was sure the bundle was in the soldier's safe keeping, she detonated the device concealed in her dress and all within five feet of her, decimated, as shrapnel and metal shards hit the soldiers, tearing away flesh and body armour. Body parts and limbs flew into the air like flesh twigs as bodies crumbled into the ground and what was once a living breathing man, was now just a piece of burnt meat with its insides ripped apart, his flesh and bones arrayed like confetti decorating the ground. The corporal had christened the bones of his victims 'flesh twigs' because when you stood on them they snapped, like twigs. Now, his own flesh twigs lay scattered and discarded from his once proud body.

The shocked, blood-splattered soldiers remaining, emptied their weapons into the cars and lorries where the woman had come from, continuing to shoot until their guns were empty, the hatred for their enemy only appeased by their fingers on the triggers.

Richard, stunned and numb looked on, as tears began to fill his eyes, but he could not or dare not weep. He checked that Hancock was not looking as he quickly wiped the tears away with his cloth handkerchief. Sergeant Hancock put down his binoculars, sat back and took two long swigs from his bottle of water.

Around them, silence broke into the volume of battle. For just a few seconds, the only noise they could hear was the crackling of fire and breaking of glass as the heat expanded, turning it back to liquid.

For an hour or more Richard and Hancock sat in their observation position, few words passing between them.

One of the American soldiers moved towards them, Hancock stood to acknowledge him. 'We are just here to observe, Lieutenant. Is it all clear now?' He saluted firmly, the salute returned.

'Sure is.' Richard was not sure what accent he had but it sounded Southern States. 'If you want to come and take a look-see be our guest, but be careful, there may be a couple of those fuckers still anxious to take someone out. So stay frosty.'

Hancock got up, smoothed his uniform down with his hands, picked up his SA80, and headed down towards the centre of the column. Richard followed closely behind, the safety off on his weapon, ready to fire.

It was late evening before the Jeep rolled back into the base camp, one which had already started to empty out. Richard climbed out of the Jeep and headed back to his tent, his head, hands, jacket, and boots all caked in dirt, blood, and sand. Without ceremony, he tumbled onto the bed, burying his face in the pillow, his body exhausted and drained.

Minutes later, he dragged his body up off the bed, as he heard a noise outside.

Peter walked into the tent, beaming, in his hand a large bottle of red wine, with no label. 'Richard. Richard! Hey, you okay? Listen, I just heard we're shipping out in a couple of days. Hey, what's up? Hey…'

Not looking at Peter, Richard got off his cot, sat on the edge, and stared at his reflection in the shaving mirror opposite him on the makeshift table, made from a crate labelled spare parts. His face was dirty and creased by sweat, looking as if he had aged ten years, his head covered in a thick grey dust.

Peter, lost for words, held up the bottle and waved it at him, then realised the folly of that suggestion. Richard's expression was empty of emotion. 'Oh God, mate, I'm sorry. You were on observation duty today. I forgot. How did it go?' Peter leaned across the crate and picked up a green apple and began to polish it against his uniform.

Richard turned to Peter, his expression somewhat quizzical. 'Peter, do you remember where you were when Chapman shot John Lennon?'

'Yes, I was in London, Shaftesbury Avenue. It was near Christmas so we were doing a bit of shopping when I heard. Why?'

Richard sat still and looked at him. 'I know exactly where I was, I was in the car, in Winchester on my way to meet my mates, I was fourteen and we were going to a gig that night. I remember it came on the radio, and then they kept repeating it. I remember it, because I knew it was a day that I would never forget, never.'

'Why do you ask, Rich?'

'Why, because what I saw today, I will never forget, never forget it. It will stay with me always.'

'Lennon being shot was terrible, I agree, but this is war, war. You know the drill, Rich. It's what we are here for.'

Richard stood up and looked straight at Peter. His eyes were full of sorrow, yet there was deep anger and contempt for his friend at that moment for the way that he had just made that statement. 'You think what I saw today was WAR?' His voice rose in volume. 'You want to call this war, because it's convenient, so tell me where is the glory then, Pete, where are the medals and the battles? If this is war... where are the heroes? This was no war... this was murder, pure cold-blooded murder, slaughter.'

'I don't know what you saw, nor do I want to know but it's them or us, man. It's the way it has always been; kill or be killed. We didn't write the rules; we just carry out the orders. It's never going to be pretty!'

'You think I am that naïve that I don't know the difference between war and murder? But you weren't there, and I appreciate that. You want me to tell you what it was like, I don't know if I can... How can I even begin to describe it, as I have never seen anything like it? Even now I can still smell the stench of burnt flesh. Still taste the acrid smoke as it choked my lungs. Still see the empty eyes of the dead soldiers, as they lay crumpled in their vehicles, as the road burned...'

Peter sat down; listening to Richards's heartfelt words, holding the apple in his hand, turning it round and round in his fingers.

'I have never seen such destruction, such terror, such horror. I watched it all and I did nothing…' Richard picked up a bottle of water and drank from it.

Peter watched the agony in Richard's eyes, seeing his friend relive every minute of the day.

'You know, a woman killed herself before my eyes. She blew herself up just to kill an American soldier. I think she blew her baby up too… I never thought I would see…' Richard stopped and replayed the scene in his mind, seeing the woman again, as she handed the baby to the US Corporal. He drank again, taking a longer gulp, and swallowed the cold liquid down. 'I actually thought... I thought I'd get through this without a scratch. Fuck! I know I have no divine right to say that. Why should I? It's part of my job, right? Dying! But today, this wasn't a job, it wasn't even part of being a soldier, this was slaughter, cold-blooded murder, disguised as war, and as I sat there watching, and listening, I wondered what it must have been like to be in that column of 2,000 vehicles and thousands of people. TRAPPED, unable to move, unable to go back, or forward. Men, women and children locked together in one line of despair and terror, with nowhere to run, or hide, just one long straight road to oblivion. Practice targets for an unseen enemy, picked off without thought for whom or what was killing them.'

'They chose to fight, mate. They could have surrendered. Most of the others did.'

'Chose surrender... You think so? They had no choice in this, no choice at all.' Richard turned to Peter. His eyes started to itch and he wiped them with the cloth he used to clean his Panda look. 'Ok, possibly they were the Republican Guard or maybe they were just conscripts given guns and forced to shoot at us. But what is our protocol? We shoot back, kill, or be killed you said. Regardless! And for what, most of those people were trying to escape it all! I saw dead mothers, holding and clutching their dead sons to their breasts as if they were children. I saw soldiers in their trucks and in the convoy, burnt alive, their heads etched into the metal of their vehicles moulded together in steel and flesh, twisted wrecks of humanity unrecognisable as a name or a person…' Richard paused, picked up the bottle of water and held it in his hand. Trying to stop his welling eyes, he wiped the cloth against the sweat and tell-tale tears. 'After the bombing stopped and it was all over we got up from our sanctuary and I walked among them. And it was then I had the weirdest feeling. I felt like I was in a gallery, the pieces all part of a great exhibition, as if each person was an exhibit, displayed and captured in that moment, their death framed for all to see. And among all that wanton carnage, there was one abiding image that will stay with me always. Out of all the horrors I saw, a woman lay dead next to a young soldier; she had her arms clutched around his neck as if she was embracing him, cradling him to her. She was obviously his Mother, the one who had brought him into the world and now she was with him as he left it. In that moment, the two most significant events in that boy's life were captured and framed for all to see, the one who gave him life, the place where it ended, and she was there with him.'

Peter leans across to his friend; seeing the pain in Richard's eyes. 'Richard, whatever happened today, happened for a reason. Be thankful you came through it okay. I am, man! You could easily be lying there, on that road, next to them.'

'Yes, you're right of course.' Richard looked down to the floor and across to his friend. His anger mellowed. 'But... they were running away. From what though? From us, Saddam and his deadly regime, or from life itself? Where were they going, Peter? Sixty miles of highway with only one destination at the end of it, an uncertain future.' Richard paused, opened the bottle, and sipped the last drop of water from the bottle. 'But we saved them that trouble, didn't we? We gave them no future at all. We ended it for them, there on that road.' Richard sat back on the bed and looked to his friend, his eyes glazed with tears. 'I know what you're saying... I am a soldier too, a soldier, not a killer. I value life, but I know that if I had to protect myself, my family, my fellow soldiers, I would kill. But today... today I felt ashamed I was a soldier. I felt ashamed that I was a human being. I felt ashamed I was alive to see this.'

'Richard, you did what you had to do. You are alive, ashamed, or not. There were killers among them, rapists, and murderers. People who would not be thinking like you are now. They wouldn't think twice about putting a bullet between your eyes. You said a woman killed herself. She had no thought for herself or her baby. Her doctrine was to kill a Yankee soldier. Did she show pity for the soldier? Did she show any other thought for him or his family? He too was just doing his job. I can tell you now for nothing, they would not feel ashamed of doing it either! They would gloat over such an act of defiance. It's their culture to do so. Now you must forget it and put it to the back of your mind. We are going home soon. It's over, Richard. It's over.'

Richard sat back on the bed, 'Is it? You think just because I close my eyes it will all go away?'

'No, I do not. I never said it would. But if you don't at least think of something else, it will make you ill. You've got to snap out of it. It's over! Try and get some sleep. You have had a bad day. Let's just keep it to the one day, yeah? Go see the Doc, get some pills, some *tranqs* sleeping pills, anything to get you out of these thoughts. I don't know, I'm no expert but you need to distance yourself from this. Ok, now, I better get back to the unit, we will open this bottle tomorrow when you are feeling better.'

Richard stretched his hand out to shake Peter's. 'Sure, and thanks.'

'No problems. I'd better go. Just try to rest, mate.' Peter left the tent.

Left to his thoughts, Richard couldn't think of anything else other than what he saw that day, so he picked up the book he had already read from cover to cover and fingered the pages. On the side of the made-up table was a small bottle of sleeping tablets. He took one, swallowed it without water and let it dissolve on his tongue, the after-taste seeming bitter as he continued to read.

Richard looked at the bottle again, opens it and took two more tablets. The after-taste was just the same as before. He dropped the book onto his chest and slowly drifted off. But his sleep was disturbed as he wrestled with the images of the day.

He opened his eyes, outside sirens wailed and voices cried out, explosions rang around the camp.

Private Jones rushed into the tent covered in blood; his stomach open, pulsing thick dark scarlet blood. He staggered towards Richard screaming. 'They're coming, get out!!!'

Richard rose from the bed and hurriedly put on his boots, picked up his rifle, exited the tent, and started running, in no particular direction. As he ran he noticed the camp was strafed with bullets. Richard ran towards the floodlights ahead of him to finally emerge on HIGHWAY 80. He raced past several of the vehicles and the faces of dead soldiers and civilians in a nightmare vision. Richard kept running and found himself standing amidst the devastation and carnage!

A woman dressed in black walked slowly towards him through the smoke, and as she drew nearer, he could tell she wore the scent of death. Beside him, the woman from earlier knelt close to him, gripped a grenade, pulled the pin, lifted the bundle towards him then raised her veil. He saw her face clearly for the first time. She had no eyes. Richard waited, unable to move then he heard a different woman's voice calling to him. 'Come Richard, come to me now.' It was softly spoken almost like a song.

Richard turned to the new voice and began to run towards it through the smoke and dust. He emerged on a shore, the sea rolling in around him, where all was still, except for the noise of the waves as they broke onto the beach. He looked out to sea, as the woman who was calling to him, beckoned to him to go to her. She was naked, perfect and serene as she walked from the waters towards him.

He snapped his eyes wide open and awoke, sweating.

CHAPTER FOUR

REMEMBER, 2011

Paphos airport was not busy for a Sunday evening, as Richard and Julie collected their hired car. Their first night in Cyprus had been one of discovery in many ways. For starters, Julie had not expected the impromptu visit to Aphrodite's Rock for some pilgrimage Richard had cooked up.

He had covered up his intentions by first treating her to a good meal at Costa's Restaurant, where he and the young co-owner got into an animated conversation of origins and beginnings and sounded like they had known each other for ages. Costa was a short man, around five-foot-six, but stocky, with a trimmed black beard, and neat black hair. With dark eyes and a tanned face, which gave off a perfect sheen, as if he had polished his skin, it made him look even younger than he probably was. Subsequently, after much conviviality, an outstanding spread was offered. Still, that sneaky detour had been nothing but a cover-up for Richard's real goal; the rocks...

Not even pretending at his true purpose, Richard got up from his seat, made his way between a couple of tables—the diners ignored him, as they too were engrossed in their meals—walked around the restaurant, where posters of the Rocks adorned the walls; there was even a crudely drawn,

35

poorly painted fading mural of a Botticelli vision of the Birth of Aphrodite, behind which he discovered the side shop. The tiny spot, which was barely a hole-in-the-wall, offered dozens of figurines, pictures, and tourist trappings devoted to the Goddess. He meandered gingerly and finally picked a book of postcards, with which he made an offering to Julie, who happened to be standing beside him, as she had decided to go see what he was so engrossed with.

She too selected a souvenir, but something practical; a guide-book of the attractions with the usual English/Greek phrases which she began practicing on him. Her Greek accent mixed with Bostonian was rather curious on the ears.

After their meal, settlement of the bill, and a fond farewell to Costa, who acknowledged them with, 'come back to see us again.' Both walked outside and back to the car.

Richard seemed particularly excited and Julie put it down to the wine, but that was before he revealed as to why he had chosen this specific location.

'Jules, come with me, I want to show you something.'

'What now?'

'Five minutes, that's all, I only ask for five minutes… it's just along here.'

'What is and how do you know it is.' Julie's Bostonian twang was becoming more obvious.

'I saw the sign. Look, it's just a few minutes down the road, please?'

'Richard, I'm tired and I want my bed.' Julie's patience was running thin but sometimes it was hard to say no. 'Okay, five minutes, but that is it.'

Thankful, Richard took her by the hand as they returned to their vehicle.

They arrived on the coast road overlooking the beach quickly, the smell of sea air prominent in their nostrils. Getting out of the car, Richard steered Julie over the gravel and pebbles and down to the sandy intermittent rock-covered beach. With little light, he picked his way along the shore and together they crunched across the shingle and the smooth stones.

Julie was barely holding on to him and her temper.

Before them, silhouetted against the sea and the moonlight, was a large rock formation, a single boulder stood embedded in the sand, and behind it and slightly further out at sea were two more barely visible in the darkness.

'Here we are, Aphrodite's Rock.' Richard waved an arm in a grand arc.

'This is what you wanted to show me?' Julie couldn't contain her lack of enthusiasm.

Richard moved closer to the huge rock.

'It's a bloody rock, Richard. A Rock! Just look at it! It's huge.'

'I know, but can't you sense the mystery and magic of this place?'

'No, I can only sense the mosquitoes biting me. I have had enough, let's go.'

'Two minutes, Jules, just two minutes, as I have never been this close before. I have only ever seen it from the road or from the air.'

Julie turned and began to walk back to the steps. 'I'm going. If you're not here in two minutes, you can walk to Limassol.'

'Just another minute and I'll be with you.' Richard's smile was his alone as he walked towards the sea and offered a 'thank you' to an unseen hostess. He turned and chased after his wife, who was almost at the top of the road. The sea washed in behind him and covered his footprints. You would never know he had been there.

The stupid excursion left Julie more than a little pissed off. She just could not see what all the fuss was about. Okay, the legend said the goddess of love had been born at this location, but as she also succinctly put it one more time. 'It's a bloody rock, a big one, but a bloody rock.' Her broad Bostonian accent came to the fore when she was annoyed and it echoed off the empty beach.

Now, this! You could almost hear the incredulity in Julie's mind as she pondered Richard's next move. Peter Shaw, Richard's old Army buddy and so-called best friend of subsequent years—though neither had set eyes on the other for almost twenty—had had a five-minute phone conversation that morning and guess what, they were off again on some other adventure.

'I haven't even had time to unpack properly; half my clothes are strewn all over the bed.' She complained.

'Get dressed quick, love, I've made some coffee and toast. Black, just the way you like it and the toast is as well.'

'Oh, how funny you are, Mr. Cole.' Julie Cole, wife, mother, and lover of Richard had seen it all before. The sudden impulsive nature of Richard had always kept her on her toes. She had weathered well over the past twenty or so years since they first met, of course her body had become a little heavier, after two kids it was not easy to get back to a 20-inch waist and get into the tight-fitting jeans that used to accentuate her sexiness. But when she looked in the mirror, she couldn't help but smile, she still had it, that Julie look, even with the passing years her face was blemish free, her hair always neat, no matter what colour she made it, and whether she was a red head, blonde or brunette her tell-tale green eyes always carried in them that suggestion that there was more to her than at first glance assumed. But Richard's latest escapade had left her head spinning and she was annoyed and frustrated, with thoughts which she kept to herself. 'This was supposed to be our holiday. God knows we haven't had one for years. But since we have arrived we haven't had a minute's relaxation and now we are off again.'

Richard ushered Julie into the car. 'Okay, love, Peter said he would meet us at a place just outside Akrotiri. It's a British base so we won't be able to park inside, but he has a place for us just away from the base so we will meet him there.'

Julie just nodded, donned her designer sunglasses, and eased herself back into the passenger car seat, while adjusting her cut-down pants and letting the air conditioner cool and tease her bare legs.

Richard checked the directions on Peter's text once more on his cell and then drove off in the direction of Paphos.

Cyprus roads were fairly straightforward, no traffic to speak of, and definitely not like back home. He could never be sure when he left the house what time he would get to work. If it wasn't for traffic jams, or an accident or two or just bloody road-works that delayed him, something always did anyway. But this drive was genuinely relaxing as he headed out onto the motorway and away from town.

'He said it's about twenty-five minutes, just past Kolossi, that's where Richard the Lion Heart used to live with his Cyprus Queen Berengaria.'

'I am impressed, Richard, quite the tourist we are, aren't we? Where did you learn that?'
Julie smirked in her cool calculating way.

Richard responded in his usual matter-of-fact way. 'I did a lot of reading when I was here last and in Kuwait, just one of the things I picked up.'

'I am glad that's the only thing you picked up.' Julie smirked again hiding a wry smile.

'Julie Cole, what a terrible thing to say.' He laughed loudly and both laughed together, knowing that Richard was not the type for an affair of any description. They were as much in love with each other as they had been the first night they crept under the duvet covers away from a sudden snow storm; right in the heart of deepest Winchester all those years ago.

Peter was parked off the road, his hazard lights were on and he kept checking the rear-view mirror to see if the SBA (Sovereign Base Police) were about. He checked his watch, it was still early, just after 9:30. He had to be back in Dhekelia by 11:30 so they would have just under an hour. The phone rang in the car.

'Hello, Sheila…. Yes… okay yes… I know… take it easy then and I will. What, you are going out again? Okay, well, have fun…. See you later…' Peter could see a car approaching. 'Fine, honey, I think they are here, got to go, bye.' The car passed, it wasn't them. Peter glanced at his watch once more. The phone rang again.

'Pete, sorry, I think we took a wrong turn. I am somewhere near the Monastery of Cats or something like that... oh, not far, okay... so it's back to the main road, turn right and then follow the signs for Akrotiri, got it. Be there soon.'

Peter got out of the car and reached into his trousers to take out a pack of cigarettes, but there weren't any in the packet, Sheila had emptied them. 'Fuck, just when I wanted a smoke.' He protested to an empty road.

It was another nine minutes before Richard's car appeared. Peter was standing outside, the sun now hot and beating heavily onto his already red forehead.

Richard jumped out of the car and Julie followed slowly behind him. Richard's face beamed brightly as he held his friend firmly in a hug of companionship, the demure figure of Julie sandwiched just behind the two men. Richard's reaction was one of joy at seeing his old friend, both had grown older of course and both had changed in stature. Peter had matured his small beer belly into something best described as rotund. Richard's body in contrast was much the same as it was when they first met but his hair had begun to recede; perhaps he too had put on a few pounds, but he was in no way in the same league as Peter. But none of that mattered as the two friends hugged each other and shook hands.

'Peter, it's so good to see you... I can't believe it... you look great. This life is doing you well.... Oh shit, where's my manners? Sorry, this is Julie, my much better half.'

Julie leaned between the two and planted a kiss on Peter's cheek.

'It's so good to meet you at long last, and your pictures don't do you justice, Julie.'

'Thank you.' Julie's coy smile was glossed over as the two men reminisced. It was an odd place for a reunion but it seemed to fit the bill nicely.

'I have a surprise for you, Rich, but we need to take my car, the road is a bit rough, so leave yours here. Park it there and we will shoot off. After you, Julie,' Peter's manners were just as she would expect for an ex-pat, impeccable.

Richard parked the hired car in a shady spot just off the road.

'It will be safe there, Rich, don't worry.'

'Don't forget the camera, love.' Julie shouted back to Richard as he was shutting the car door. He opened it up again, leaned in and picked up the camera from the back seat. Julie held Peter's arm as they walked towards the 4-wheel drive. Richard scampered after them, the camera swinging around his neck. Julie clambered into the back seat whilst Richard plonked himself in the front passenger seat.

'Seat belts on guys, this is sovereign base territory, and the police are sharp here on any wrongdoing.' All belted in. 'Good, as I said, the road is a bit rough so hold tight, but we won't be more than five minutes.' Peter said as he turned the steering wheel sharply and headed down what could only be best described as a dirt road, the bumps and ruts seemingly getting bigger and bigger as the vehicle manoeuvred its way through them.

Ahead of them was a large field covered with orange trees, the crop had already been picked and only a few remnants of the harvest remained. To one side, parked in an open space away from the trees was a very smart R44 helicopter, which looked almost brand new, its paintwork shimmering in the sun.

'She's a beauty, isn't she? And we have her for an hour. So, let's get going and let's see what we see, eh guys?' Peter couldn't contain his excitement for his new toy, and was still extolling the copters' virtues as he walked swiftly across the ground and into the pilot's seat.

Julie followed excitedly.

Richard was not so swift to respond, in fact, he felt full of trepidation; this was something he had not expected, something he did not want to do but knew he had to. His last helicopter ride had led him into the beginnings of his nightmares; he had no wish for them to start again. But it would be wrong to say anything, after all, Peter had gone to a lot of trouble to arrange this, and by the way he was acting, it was almost as if what he was doing was not allowed. He climbed into the passenger seat, while Julie sat behind him. The rotors started and began to whirl and spin and the noise grew louder with every rotation.

'Ok, we have this for an hour then I have to get it back to Dhekelia. It's a training copter and sometimes we use it for scenic tours; this one is unofficial as I borrowed it, so keep it quiet, eh guys? Now it will get very loud, so if you want to say something, shout, okay?' Peter's own voice raised an octave or two as he spoke.

Julie sat in her chair, her face beaming. 'I've never been in a helicopter before, so this is great, thank you so much.' Julie smiled and tapped Peter on the back.

Richard leaned forward to peer out of the front of the craft. The blades twirled and twisted in the air as the helicopter rose higher. 'Where are we going?' He glanced across at Peter as he steered the craft.

'We are going to skirt along the coast then we will head towards Paphos and Akamas, via Aphrodite's Rock, you remember Aphrodite's Rock.'

'We have already been there, once.' Julie piped up from the back. 'It was the first thing we did. Richard said he owed a favour to a lady.'

'Enough said, love.' Richard's annoyance with his wife was clear, but the noise of the helicopter soon drowned out any further discussion.

Peter broke up the spat. 'First thing we will do is go along the coast, that way we can take a look at the Roman Villa in Curium, it looks good from the air. Get your camera ready.'

Richard turned to apologise to his wife. Next to her sat a figure, dressed in desert fatigues. It was Sergeant Hancock. Julie looked at Richard as he turned back swiftly and then turned again to check on the spectral visitor who had vanished. The copter began to turn and then rise.

The cliffs around Curium came into view as Richard picked up his camera. He lifted it to his eye expecting to see a rocky outcrop instead the lens brought forth a series of strange images. He began to click as if shooting those images, even as he could hear voices behind him.

One of those was Sergeant Hancock, and he was shouting. 'The Republican Guard are trying to get out of Kuwait, making a run for it and taking whatever they can with them, the Yanks are going to bust them open, it's our job to watch and listen. We only engage them if we have to, understood.'

Richard said nothing and kept clicking the camera, the images beginning to appear in quick succession. He could hear the blades spinning above him and he felt the craft descend rapidly. Through the lens bombs, guns and explosions could be seen in the distance.

Richard pulled back from the camera and looked at his wife, as his body began to tremble inside. He was compelled to look through the lens again. Plumes of smoke rose from the ground, as Richard felt the copter going lower and lower. He turned to see Peter holding the control stick, dressed in his pilot's gear. Richard was now deeply entrenched in this nightmare only this was not a nightmare, it was real. His surrounds magnifying his dreamlike state. He looked into the camera again.

This time, the camera picked out a road sign, Highway 80. His lens focussed on the sign and he continued to click furiously at the images unfolding in the lens, the camera now firmly trained on the Highway, which was littered with a convoy of military vehicles, buses, tanks, and personnel carriers; the wreckage of exploded vehicles, bodies of dead soldiers and some civilians littered the scene in bombed-out cars, as dead children peered through the glass of their bullet and shelled riddled buses. Air strikes continued, as more heat-seeking missiles made contact with the fleeing vehicles. Sporadic gunfire continued from inside the cars, as the insurgents fired hopelessly in the vain hope of hitting something, one of the helicopters or perhaps a tank or a vehicle that was attacking the convoy.

Peering down the lens into a scene he had witnessed before, he watched as a group of American soldiers walked towards the colony heavily armed, shooting indiscriminately at the vehicles and the people inside them. The noise in the copter grew so loud he could almost hear the explosions ringing in his ears. He pulled himself away from the camera and looked towards Julie.

She was quiet, looking out of the window at the ruins below. 'I hope you have some good shots, love, you seem to not stop clicking.' Julie said then returned to look at the vista beneath them.

Richard tried a smile but instead returned the camera to his eye. He knew what was coming next, knew what was going to happen but he couldn't stop himself, he had to look. He had to see if what had happened before would repeat itself in his lens. Pulling the camera slowly up to his eye, he began to look down into the lens. The American soldiers had strafed the buses, vans, and lorries; as more people lay limp and lifeless as the troops eased their way through the metallic chaos.

From behind a wrecked car, the woman dressed in black emerged. Richard reached his hand out, his fingers clutching emptiness. Something must be done to stop her. Was there a way to warn those ghosts, of her desire and her mission? But he couldn't, he was helpless. He simply clicked and clicked, as if the camera was his only weapon and the only way to defend them. Hoping they would hear his clicking, clicking, clicking, Richard watched as a helpless observer to memories where time itself had now slowed down and where the shadows of the past had all converged into this one scene. Even the helicopter noise has disappeared, the blades silent, nothing, no sound at all as the woman moved forward clutching her bundle in her arms, a black veil covering her face. Richard focused on her.

There was no sound as he watched her rehearsed stumble towards the troops, who stood with their guns targeted, as she drew closer. But this time as she fell to her knees and offered the bundle up, she did not offer it to the trooper, she offered it to Richard. Staring straight at him and through the lens it was as if he could feel her very breath on his face as she pulled the veil back from her face. She had no eyes, her face was white, scarred and bloody and the bundle was nothing but a clump of dirty blood-spattered rags and a skeletal figure of an infant, covered in blood and sinew as if it had already been blown apart. Richard pulled the camera back from his eye. He was shaken but hid his terror from the others, except for the tell-tale sign of his tapping foot.

'We are going to round this coast and head for Aphrodite's Rock, you can get some good shots there. Remember the first time I flew you over here?'

Richard remembered, it was the night he prayed to the goddess to bring him back safely from the war, it was also the night she responded. As they approached the familiar site of Petra Tou Romiou the craft began to descend gently. Richard leaned forward and pushed the window open to begin shooting the waters below. The edges of the waves blessed by white crests of foam rolled towards the shore as the copter drew down lower. Some people on the beach started waving to the inhabitants in the craft and Julie responded, waving back as Richard continued to shoot. The waves began to shimmer and glisten like glass as Richard pushed the camera closer to the outside.

'Careful, love, that's an expensive camera.'

Julie's warning made Richard aware of how far he had moved to get the shot. He nodded, assuring her, and then returned to shoot some more, as he focussed on the area which seemed to have less sun on it, he concentrated on his shots till he heard what he thought was a voice.

'Find me.' Was all it said.

'Sorry, Jules, did you say something?'

'No, why?'

'I thought... never mind.'

'Had enough, Rich, got all the shots you want?' Peter's short request meant that time was moving on.

Richard nodded and pointed his camera down for the last time, taking shots of the water and rocks as the helicopter hovered and the downdraught made the waves crystal clear through to the bottom.

Disturbing the moment, the radio suddenly switched on. Peter and Julie seemed oblivious to the broadcast. Richard stared at the radio, the broadcast was from 1991.

'Some estimates say that as many as 2000 lives were lost between the late hours of the 26th and 27th of February in what can only be described as a massacre. When US air and ground forces attacked, a convoy of retreating Republican guards and civilians North of Al Jahra on Highway 80. We will bring you more on this story as we get it.'

Richard stared at Peter seated in his chair for a second or two, recalling the events.

'What's up pal, we are off to Paphos now, okay?'

As the copter pulls away, Julie leans closer to the window. 'I was right it is a bloody big rock.'

Richard smiled as the helicopter veered away along the coast. Below them, two small fishing boats shuffled through the waters.

CHAPTER FIVE

A NIGHT ON THE TOWN

It was just after 10:45 when the helicopter landed back in the field. Peter, keen to get going, jumped out of the craft and ran over to the waiting 4X4. Julie and Richard, bowing their heads as the blades whizzed over them joined Peter in the 4X4.

'Thank you so much, Peter. That was fantastic.' Julie was pleased to be on the ground but also delighted with the experience.

'Yes, Pete, that was great. And again, we can't thank you enough, it's a great way to start our holiday.'

'Okay you two, I'm taking you back to your car, then scoot back here to get the lady back to Dhekelia. We can meet later, maybe go for a meal tonight, that is, unless you have something else planned. I know Sheila would be delighted to meet with you both finally. So I will send you a text where and when, okay?'

Neither Richard nor Julie said a word, just going along with the idea, as the 4 X 4 picked its way through bumps and ruts as they made their way back to their car again.

'I'll drop you guys off here and I will get a lift back from one of the boys in Dhekelia. Glad you enjoyed yourselves.' Peter said as he stopped the car.

The shaded area had kept Richard's car protected but it was still hot inside and Julie's first action was to get the air conditioning on. Richard started the car and pulled out onto the main road.

Julie let the AC tease her bare legs. 'My ass is sore, they are not the most comfortable seats those helicopters.'

Her comment made Richard smile.

'Jesus, Richard, how many shots did you take? You were like David Bailey on heat. I hope they come out okay. No thumb shots over the lens.'

Richard said nothing, but he too wondered what the camera had captured. Would the images that haunted him all those years ago, now haunt him again? How could that even be possible?

They drove back to the centre along the sea front, as their apartment complex was close to an area called Gallatex, which by day seemed quite ordinary which was true for most of Limassol's seafront, but by night when the bars, clubs and restaurants opened their doors, the city took on another image. Locals mixed with tourists and as day gave way to night the atmosphere began to electrify as the neon signs emblazoned the strip and with over 300 bars, clubs, and restaurants to choose from there was plenty of choice in cuisine as well as entertainment.

From their apartment balcony, Julie could watch the sea as it washed along the shoreline, even with the sun going down people were still swimming and there were even a few last-minute stragglers eager to get a few rays of extra dwindling sunshine. Julie sat, coffee cup in hand as Richard joined her. They sat together watching the action below.

'Finally,' Julie said and sipped from her cup. 'This is the first chance we've had to rest or relax, we don't seem to have had a minute of our own, not that the helicopter ride wasn't fantastic, but it is after all our holiday. I can't even remember our last one.'

'I can, it was Spain. We went to Benidorm, Matthew was sick on the plane, and I got Spanish tummy and had the shits for about four days. I recall that holiday well.' Richard smiled.

'That's right, and Molly lost her doll and we had to go from one end of the beach to the other to find it, we never did and she was so upset I ended up having to buy her another one, but when we went in the shop she didn't want that, she wanted that bloody donkey, which she still has displayed on her bedside cabinet gathering dust. Now I remember Spain.' Julie leaned over and kissed her husband.

'What's that for?' Richard seemed surprised.

'Just because I love you and this is our holiday, together, and really our first night.'

'Well, Mrs. Cole, if you mean what I think you mean, please adjourn with me to the bedroom.'

Julie smiled then giggled then turned away and made her way to the bedroom. The cell phone rang.

'Hello, oh, hi Pete, no, no, we are fine, got back okay, went for a bite to eat and just spent the rest of the day resting. Tonight? Yes. Well, let me check with Julie, hold on...'

Julie said nothing, she just closed the door behind her to the bedroom.

'She said she would love to, Pete. Yes, it would be great to meet Sheila. About eight then, yes... Make it 8:30, give us a bit of time to shower, change and get ready... ok, send me a text and we'll meet you there. No, we'll get a taxi… no problem… Great, and we'll see you there then. Bye.' Richard, clicked the cell off, and walked slowly towards the bedroom. He pushed the door open.

Julie stood naked in front of him.

'I should have made it nine o'clock.' He said as he closed the door behind him softly.

Peter sat down on the sofa, picked up the cell phone, and began to text Richard.

Sheila went to sit down beside him and placed two mugs of hot tea on the coffee table in front of her. 'You had a good day then, where did you go?'

'I borrowed one of the choppers for an hour and took them for a spin over the coast.'

Sheila stood up, her body straight.

She was much taller than Peter and as if to prove it she always wore heels, just to make that difference obvious. She was also two years younger, a fact she always reminded him of. Perhaps it was her height or her age or just her general demeanour, but she always looked down on him in many ways. Peter had grown older by comparison and it showed, whilst Sheila had tried to maintain her looks. For the most part, it worked. Her make-up was always just right, had even taken courses in it to be sure of that. It was part of Sheila's nature to be 'Miss Perfect' and she worked hard at it, even her wardrobe of clothes smacked of designer labels, perhaps the odd concession to Marks and Sparks but generally it was Gucci, Channel, Louis Vuitton, and Michael Kors, a personal favourite. As Peter watched, it wouldn't have mattered what she was wearing today, it was the expression on her face that said it all and her words followed.

'Why did you do that, you know you are not supposed to use those machines for private use. Fuck me, Peter, we are struggling hard enough as it is and now you go and jeopardise what little cash we have coming in by possibly losing your job. And to top it all, you make a booking for an expensive restaurant with your army buddy, whom I have never met or wanted too, just a few Christmas cards over the years, but suddenly we are bosom pals. Fuck me, Peter, you are priceless.' Sheila's anger was tempered but the venom in her words was obvious, because even when she was angry she showed complete control. Never once did she raise her voice, just kept it mellow, but vicious.

Peter watched her rich brown eyes, which were really the only element of her person that stayed constant, as the song went, 'She's got Bette Davis eyes.' Her hands gesticulated, but her eyes never blinked as she spoke. There was no doubt Sheila was a good-looking woman for her age; she had kept herself trim with lots of exercises, some she kept very private. Still standing, she glanced in the large glass mirror above the fireplace and passed her fingers lightly through her blonde hair, only finite wisps of grey hair interrupting her blonde look, her favourite style of the moment. This attention to detail and her pure selfishness for personal perfection made her feel good, Sheila loved herself.

She sat back down on the sofa. 'We can't afford to do this, Peter, but I suppose you have made the promise now...' her tone had mellowed. 'But I don't want you leaving me there on my own with her, I am not going to be some excuse so you can drink and talk army, do you understand?' In just one sentence the venom had returned.

'Would I do that to you?' Peter's words verged on the sarcastic, but his smile and soft kiss on her cheek made it clear he understood what she meant.

Sheila picked up her mug of tea took two further sips and left it on the table. 'I will go shower and get ready.'

'I will come and join you, we have a few hours yet.'

'No, you won't, those days are over. Drink your tea and watch some TV.'

Peter's attempt at sex was dismissed in one sentence. His sex life had been non-existent for some time and it wasn't middle age or brewer's droop as they used to call it, it was simply that Sheila didn't love him anymore. They stayed together purely for financial reasons, as they couldn't sell the house although it was on the market and neither could afford to move out. It was the classic love stalemate. Peter did as he was told and switched the TV on then flicked through the channels till he found something to watch, which was a repeat of a cooking programme he had already watched earlier in the week.

The crumpled bedroom sheet betrayed the events of the early evenings' passion. Julie awoke from her sleep and with her eyes still shut she fumbled on the bed for her husband. He wasn't there. She woke properly and looking around the room saw just the stacked cases and a cold cup of coffee on the bedside table. 'Richard, Richard,' she called out to him.

'I'm out here.' He said from the balcony.

Julie lay back on the bed and settled for five more minutes before she decided to get up.

Richard was reading the Cyprus Guide Book Julie had bought the night before at the restaurant whilst drinking his freshly made coffee. The sun was already down so he wore a pair of long shorts, his only protection against the evening breeze. His skin had grown accustomed to sunlight over the years, but still he had taken the necessary sun-block precautions to save himself from burning and spoiling the holiday.

From the balcony, he had a good view of the beach, which was emptying rapidly. He would rise early tomorrow to get a prime position, he knew how busy the beach could get and he had already selected the spot. He sipped his coffee and returned to his book.

Julie joined him. She was wearing a towelling bath robe and as she sat next to her husband, it opened to her thighs.

Richard smiled and gave his wife a loving kiss. 'It says here that Aphrodite's Rock was a haven for orgies and hedonistic behaviour and a cult grew up around the legend.'

'No wonder you're so fascinated. Lust and debauchery is just your thing before dinner or breakfast.' Julie teased.

'It also says that the Baths of Aphrodite in Polis outside of Paphos was the place where she went to regain her virginity after every conquest. There she would entertain and play with her lovers in the cool waters of this secluded cove.'

'Well, she's lucky. Unfortunately, for the rest of us, once we lose it, we lose it, and we can't get it back.' Julie smiled sarcastically.

'Coffee?' Richard poured Julie a cup, which she drank black, because as she put it, it was *the American way.* He offered her the cup and returned to reading.

'I will go finish unpacking and get ready. So what is the plan for tonight then? You know this place better than me.'

'I wasn't here that long we only did a couple of pub runs. Besides, Peter says we are to meet him at this tavern in Zygi. It's supposed to be very good.'

'Why don't you finish your coffee and have a shower. In the meantime, we need milk and food, as we haven't got anything except those odd bits in the fridge, so we need to stock up. I'm going out to see which shops are around here, after that I will get ready, okay? And it's still early we can ring Molly when I get back, at Simon's.' Julie finished her coffee and stood close to the balcony.

'Great, leave me here. I will finish this, clean up and get ready.'

'All right, see you in a little while.' She kissed her husband lightly on his lips before she left the apartment.

Richard picked up his coffee cup to drink the last remnants then busied himself about the apartment, before returning to the balcony to watch the sun dropping down to the sea.

Julie had quickly acclimatised herself to the local surroundings and had found a shop that sold English newspapers and the groceries she needed. She also found a local bakery that offered an array of delicious cakes and breads to die for, all home-baked. The variety for such a small place was good and she also chose a tray of pastries to go with the Greek bread and loaves. Returning to the apartment she passed a number of small tourist-trap shops that sold all sorts of curios and paraphernalia, most of which carried a Cypriot symbol on them, or some crude reference to what you could do on the island or what had been done to them.

Julie's window-shopping led her to one particular store that appeared to cater to collectors of Greek Mythology figures, mostly of Aphrodite in all her various poses, some with arms, others without, as featured in classic sculptures. But these porcelain, china, or even chalk mass-manufactured figures were on the cheap and nasty side and lacked finesse; but one wouldn't think so from the price labels attached to them. In the mind of the shopkeeper, Aphrodite was a big tourist attraction, though not a particularly profitable one, judging from the number of pieces left unsold.

Finding her way back upstairs to the apartment as the lift was not working, she met with Richard just as he had finished in the shower, only a white beach towel covering him.

'Jules, get everything we need?'

'Yes, got some nice cakes and bread, some beer too, and an English paper. What time are we due to be there?'

'I said about eight thirty. It's just seven now so we have tons of time. Pass us the paper.'

Julie handed it to him, which was the day's edition. He picked it up and moved over to the small sofa and lay down to read. Julie disappeared into the bathroom.

Richard scanned the paper, there wasn't that much in it, except for more problems in Syria and Iraq, more innocent people killed or wounded, more problems in the Eurozone, with more pressure on the PM. He put the paper down, time to get ready. As he stood to walk back to the bedroom, he could hear the shower running and as he selected his clothes he heard just the faintest whisper, as if someone was standing behind him and whispering in his ear, 'find me'. He looked quickly behind him, nothing, his imagination was again in overdrive.

He picked his way through the suitcase and noticed that his light weight chinos, the ones he planned to wear were creased to buggery and he had no iron with which to sort it out, so they were off the menu. Instead, he opted for a pair of navy blue serge trousers, a checked black and red short-sleeve shirt, a smart grey jacket, and blue sneakers. He dressed and waited for his wife, checking the mirror to see that he was properly attired for a night on the town.

The door to the bedroom opened and Julie walked in. The little black dress looked great on her, working extremely well with her light brown hair. Her natural blonde had vanished over the years and a succession of colourants had perfected the Julie look. She still liked short trimmed hair, but she gave in to Richard's request to grow it a little longer. Her make-up was also perfectly applied. It was a skill she had grown good at and she was now able to adapt her look automatically, not only in her dress sense, but in her facial appearance too. Not too much and not too little, just the correct amount of mascara and eyeshadow and always the right shade of lipstick, sometimes rich and ruby, other times subtle and sophisticated. When she went out, which wasn't often, she appeared the part. Her jewellery of a silver encrusted rose necklace completed the look for tonight.

The taxi was early and its repetitive horn signalled its arrival. Richard picked up the keys for the apartment and they left. The driver noticed Julie immediately. Richard could see the admiration in the man's face. He knew his wife was special, and now a total stranger appreciated that too. They climbed into the back of the Mercedes, and Richard handed the driver a scrap of paper with the name of the venue. The man nodded recognition and the car gunned away. The jolt took both back-seat passengers by surprise and they quickly buckled up.

The Mercedes taxi sped down the tourist strip and out along the highway. It overtook several cars all at once, or so it seemed. It passed some of the hotels they had seen earlier, which were brightly lit with signs that proudly displayed their names. The speed of the Mercedes was increasing as they passed a sign showing Governor's Beach on the Larnaca Nicosia highway. They overtook one more lorry in the fast lane, slowed down before taking the next exit. Zygi, five kilometres, the signpost said as they flashed past it.

As they came off the highway, the road changed to a single lane. Small pockets of houses straddled both sides of the road, as they entered the small town. *Welcome to Zygi* an English sign announced the name and greeting. The Mercedes slowed down, searching for the right place; it travelled another quarter of a mile before pulling off to the opposite side of the road. In front of a large courtyard, several more Mercedes were parked. Only these did not carry a taxi sign on them.

The driver had not spoken. He just signalled with his hands fifteen Euros. Richard handed him a blue twenty Euro note, thinking a five Euro tip was enough for his trouble. As the door shut, the taxi driver mouthed some obscenity, which sounded like 'Malacca'. He was not pleased with the tip and sped off with tires screeching against the road, scarring it with tread.

Richard draped his arm around Julie as they walked towards the restaurant along the small paved harbour walkway to breathe in the fresh evening air. It was so raw and so pure. The small harbour housed several fishing boats that had moored ready for their early morning departure. They walked past them, most of the names alluding to girls' names and some in Greek. Richard and Julie approached the restaurant door; where the sea air perfumed its entrance. Richard swung the large wooden door open to see Peter standing at the bar.

Peter shook hands with Richard, this movement introduced Julie and Sheila and together the four stood at the bar united in their welcome. This meeting was something special for all of them, communications over the past twenty odd years or so had been sketchy to say the least, and it was only after Richard decided to bring Julie to Cyprus that the conversations began, now they were all making up for lost time as if they were bosom buddies.

The restaurant too was something special. It was a celebrated fish eatery with a respected reputation for serving the finest dishes. Their *mezedes*, which were naturally fish courses, were the talk of the town, as they offered a platter and plethora of various fresh catches that filled the plates.

The wines that accompanied such delicacies were international, usually white and well chilled. The restaurant's cellar was vast and lacked little in vintages. Expensive though the place was, Richard never thought twice about what he should order, Julie too loved fish and she was looking forward to this, their first real Cypriot meal.

The restaurant on the first night had been good at the rocks, but was more international and the lunch they had today was tourist fayre. This was going to be something distinctive.

The waiter took the order for the drinks and they toasted each other for the first time before all four moved over to a corner table. Julie sat opposite Richard and Peter did likewise with Sheila. There was a buzz of conversation starting almost as soon as they sat down.

'Can you speak Greek, Peter?' Julie asked.

'Yes, not too bad. I know when they are talking about me and I know when they're swearing at me. But as Sheila says, they nearly all speak English, so you won't have any problem communicating. Okay, let's get some drinks. Wine for the ladies and beer for us, eh Rich? Keo or Carlsberg for you, Rich?'

'Keo, please,'

A young waiter dressed in a smart white open-necked shirt and black waistcoat and matching trousers and black shoes waited by the table to take the order.

'*Thelo Keo, parakallo*, and a large bottle of Chianti, for the ladies.'

Richard, suitably impressed, turned to Peter. 'You do speak it well.'

'So here's a phrase for you to learn, Richard.' Peter smiled as he leant forward to instruct Richard. His eyes bright and his smile beaming, as if he was about to laugh. '*Zen milau Ellinika poli kala.*'

'What does that mean?' Julie was as interested as Richard.

'I don't speak Greek, very well.'

Richard tried to repeat what Peter had just said. '*Zen, millo... Elli...*'

Peter helped him. '*Ellinika poli kala.*'

Richard repeated it. '*Elinik* b*oli kala.*'

'Good, just keep practicing that.' Peter chuckled as Richard tries to repeat the words.

The waiter returned with the drinks. Sheila moved her glass to one side allowing for the bottles to be positioned. Peter and Richard picked up the large beer bottles and poured the golden liquid into their glasses.

Sheila turned to Julie. 'What have you seen so far, Julie?'

'Well, we have been to town and had a look round. Oh, and the helicopter ride was fantastic.'

'Yes, I heard about the helicopter ride, he hasn't taken me up yet so you must feel very privileged.' Sheila smiled.

Julie smiled too but felt awkward by Sheila's comment. 'We flew over Aphrodite's Rock. That's the second time we have been there as Richard likes the place, I think.'

It was now Richard's turn to feel embarrassed and awkward.

'What do you want to go there for? Why, it's just a bloody rock with some silly legend.' Sheila dismissed the trip as pointless.

Julie nodded slightly, agreeing with her sentiment.

The waiter poured the Chianti. Sheila tasted it and gave her approval then sipped slowly, as she watched the other three as they chatted.

Julie picked up her glass and held it up to chink her glass against Sheila's.

Richard did likewise with his and offered the toast. 'Cheers all, good to see you and thank you for making our holiday so far memorable.'

Peter smiles and joined in with his own toast, 'Welcome to CYPRUS.'

A second waiter stopped any further discussion, placing a selection of crudités on the table. They consisted of courses of pickles and carrots and some spiced vegetables. As they ate, drank, and chatted, another waiter returned with another round of drinks, and another toast was proposed. This one 'to old friends' the words spoken were heart-felt and genuine and the atmosphere grew more affectionate as the evening wore on.

Julie turned away from the men and began to chat to Sheila. 'You like it here then?'

'Cyprus? Yes, where we are in Pissouri. It's very British. I know the island is Greek-speaking but everyone seems to speak English. We can speak the language, but we don't need to, much. I learnt it pretty quickly and the kids are both bilingual now.'

'It would have been nice to say hello to them.'

'Well, you know what kids are like. They want to be off on their own as soon as they can. Stephen has a group of friends they call a *barrea*, and they've been together since school. They are always off windsurfing, or doing something on the water. Comes from living on an island I suppose. Lucy, my youngest, well, she has her own life now, she's living and working in London, wants to be a stockbroker, I think. I know she was thinking about it. What about your kids?'

Julie smiled and waits for her cue. 'Our two, Matthew is twenty-two, has a new girl almost every month, seems he just can't settle. And Molly is twenty-one. She's the adventurer, wants to go on a round-the-world trip but needs to finish UNI first. She's studying history and English literature, doing her Masters.'

'Around the world? Aren't you worried?'

'Of course, but she's also level-headed and I don't think we could stop her anyway. Besides, we will just encourage her. That way she makes her own mind up and may not go. If you just say no they might rebel, you know how it works.'

'Yes, I do, and I think it's true in adults too, cheers.' Sheila chinks glasses with Julie, the two women were getting on well.

By the third and fourth *mezedes* course, the table was starting to become crowded. Dishes piled up from one end to the other. Bits of shrimps and prawns as well as the odd mussel and scallop shell littered the table. Sheila sank another glass of white wine without a second thought. Peter continued to fill Richard's glass and added to his own well-cultured beer belly, another beer. It was clear; they were, on the surface, having a good life out here.

The room swelled with a heady mix of great food and drink. A troupe of four Cypriot musicians surrounded the table and began to serenade the party. It was authentic Greek music of the village variety, not that of the pop culture that they heard so often on the airwaves in the taverns and bars. No, this was the music of the mountains and its solid balance of authentic rhythms and instruments, made the evening truly memorable. It also added another component to the party; that of dance, as a young Cypriot girl, who was probably no more than eighteen, dressed in full traditional costume began to move around the dance floor, which was just a partitioned square in the centre of the room. She swayed in harmony to the music, slowly moving her feet and arms. The dance was not one that you could categorise easily. It wasn't a Waltz or a Foxtrot or even a belly dance. It was more a sway, her hips moving in parity with her arms, as if she were caught in a light breeze, and there was a smile on her face. She must have done this a thousand times before, but she still kept her movements fresh. She introduced a handkerchief or a short silk scarf into the dance and waved it in the air above her head. The light from the chandelier caught the fabric and it became transparent. Then with a change in chord and tempo she began to speed her dance up, first twisting then twirling and with a rousing chorus of 'HEY' from the musicians she jumped into the air and knelt.

The applause was spontaneous and the girl waved and thanked her patrons as she left the centre of the stage. The chorus of approval from Peter and Richard echoed for a few seconds more and Julie's contented smile meant only one thing, the holiday was going great.

As the two men walked to the bar, Peter moved forward beside Richard. 'Rich, when we were in the copter today, you seemed very preoccupied, and never seemed to have your fingers off the camera, were you nervous about the trip?'

'To be honest, I wasn't expecting a helicopter ride. The last time I was on one was the Gulf War and we know what happened then. I had nightmares for weeks after, so today came as a surprise. But it was a good one, and Julie loved it.'

'And now, any more nightmares?'

'No, thankfully.' Richard lifted his glass to Peter and both drank the beer quickly before ordering another one.

Over their shoulders, the two girls were busy chatting at the table while they sat at the bar, for a few more drinks, their chat mostly army and fairly basic.

As the last courses were placed on the table, there really was no more space to place either the dishes, or the food into their stomachs. Crude as that description was, they just wanted to relax, rest, and sleep. Eating had made them tired.

'Your home is not far?' enquired Julie.

'Pissouri, it's near to Paphos,' Sheila explained. 'It has its own little community, mostly *Brits* but there are others. A couple of Scandinavian families, some Germans, and of course Russians, plus some locals; it's all very tight and neat, really. We are not in and out of each other's doors, but on occasions we meet up.'

'That does sound nice. I think you need something like that especially when you're not in your own country.' Julie continued sipping her white wine and poured the rest into Sheila's glass.

'Yes, but as I said, we aren't in and out of each other's houses. We just meet up when we want to, the boys play golf a lot at Aphrodite Hills or Happy Valley. They have such wonderful facilities there and not just for the men.'

'Really?' Julie's eyes lit up at the prospect.

'At Aphrodite Hills, there's a gorgeous spa. It has the most fabulous treatments in mud and oils and one remedy that they use is with hot stones. Haven't tried that yet, but it sounds exotic, doesn't it?'

Julie nodded her approval.

Richard checked his watch, the time was getting on and as none of them could eat anymore or even drink anything else it was time for carriages. 'Peter, we had better start to make a move. We can share a taxi to get home.' Richard offered his friend a lift.

'It's ok, Rich, we are staying here tonight. There's a great hotel just down the road. Besides, I am in Dhekalia early tomorrow, I have a meeting. Why don't you stay over tonight at the hotel too? It's not that expensive.'

'Thanks, but no, we'll go back to the apartment. We don't have anything with us, not even a toothbrush.'

'They have toothbrushes at the hotel.'

'No, honestly we'll go back. In fact, we had better start making a move now. Can the waiter order us a taxi?' Richard smiled at his friend who seemed a little disappointed that the party was ending.

'One more drink then?'

'Ok, just one more.'

Peter motioned to the barman and he returned two glasses of a see-through liquid. 'Try this. You drink it down in one.' He handed the glass to Richard. Together they downed the contents in one movement.

'Whoa, what is that?' Richard was almost gasping for breath.

'Zivania. It's the local specialty of the island, like moonshine. Or at least it was until they legalised it.'

'It's like fire water.'

'Yes, they use it for everything here. They even rub it on their bodies to keep the colds and flu away, or if they have muscles that ache.'

'And they drink it too?'

'Of course, another?'

'No thanks. I want to walk out of here. I did have something to ask you, did you ever keep in contact with anyone from the Gulf?'

'Not really. We were going to have a get-together, but it got cancelled as one of the sergeants topped himself, hung himself he did, in his attic.'

'Who was that?'

'I think they said the name was Hancock. You knew him, didn't you? He was one of yours I think; surprised you didn't hear about it, it was in some of the papers too.'

Richard looked shaken and stuttered his words just a fraction as he asked the waiter to bring their bill. And still dazed, he reached for his wallet.

Peter pushed his hand away. 'No way, Richard, you're our guests. I will get this.'

Still stunned by the knowledge that Hancock had killed himself, Richard tried to make small talk as he grappled with his wallet. 'Let's split it.'

'No, this is our treat. You can get the next one.' Peter placed a wad of notes on the silver tray. The bill had come to about one-hundred-and-fifty Euros for all four of them, including the drinks.

Richard quickly converted the sum to Pounds. A night out in England would not have been cheaper, or as filling.

Sheila stood a little unsteady on her feet due to drink, moved across to Julie, hugged her and then turned to

Richard, planting a rather large kiss on both of his cheeks. Peter grinned and Julie hiccupped. They all laughed together. They had all spent a great time as they opened the large door and stepped outside.

The taxi horn sounded, as the night air hit them. Then sounded again, as they jostled for space, they kissed and thanked their hosts one more time.

Peter took Richard by the hand. 'If you're not busy tomorrow, I will pick you guys up. See if we can find those diving sites you wanted to see.'

'Make it late morning I think we will be laying in tomorrow. But thanks again for everything, goodnight. Kali something.'

'Kalinihxta, to you too.' Peter smiled and tapped his friend on the shoulder and put him in the taxi.

Julie and Richard climbed into the back of the taxi. The driver was not the same as earlier, but he did have one similar trait to the earlier one. He drove fast too.

Peter smiled as he waved the taxi away and watched it disappear around the corner.

Sheila took Peter by the arm and with her fingers pinched him hard. She had sobered up very quickly and her annoyance showed on her face.

Peter, worse-for-wear because of the drink failed to react to Sheila's hard pinch. She did it again, and this time he definitely felt it. 'Oww, fuck, that hurt.'

'I told you not to leave me on my own, didn't I?'

'Ok, ok, it's just that I haven't seen him in years,' his words fumbled from his mouth. 'And we had things to talk about, that's all. Oh, and tomorrow I'm going to take them out for the day.'

'Don't ask me to come. I've got things to do. Let's just go now.' Sheila bent down to scratch the back of her leg and rubbed her heel. 'My feet are killing me in these heels.'

Once inside the apartment, Julie kissed Richard and he returned it, his hands and mind also busy. Julie was completely relaxed, a symptom of too much drink and a feeling of contentment. She didn't feel Richard's hand as it moved to the back of her neck and pulled the zipper slowly down. The little black dress had done its job for the night, before it fell to the floor. Julie stepped slowly out of it and into the realms of passion as Richard played with her body. He kissed her slowly on the lips. She opened her mouth and their tongues met.

Julie knew all the signs, he wanted to make love and she was willing, only, she wanted to shower first, so passion had to wait, as she hoped the water might sober her up somewhat, she collected her dress and scuttled into the bedroom wearing just her bra and panties, leaving Richard with a tantalising message. 'I know what you want, I'm going to shower and then we can.'

Richard, tried to grab her to bring her closer to him, but missed as she vanished into the bedroom, leaving him rocking about on his feet as the room was just beginning to rock with him. 'Good idea, I will sit here and wait for you to shower.' His comment was to an empty room. 'I'm just going to…' He never finished his sentence, instead, he plonked himself down at the small wooden dining table, switched on the laptop, placed the camera against the side of the laptop, and began to download the pictures he had taken earlier that day. It would take a while, just long enough he thought, for Julie to shower and for him to get over his inebriated state.

CHAPTER SIX

SHE IS THERE

Richard waited until the screen opened on the desktop. The camera had surprisingly downloaded quickly and he pushed his finger around the touch pad onto the icons he had selected and began to download them.

In the bedroom, Julie had unceremoniously dispatched her underwear, her bra cast with her panties to the corner of the room. She looked around for the bath towel and wrapped herself in it as she entered the bathroom to shower. *'I think I'd better make this shower slightly cold, wake me up a bit.'* She thought to herself.

Earlier, she had called Molly who informed her that Uncle Simon was taking them all out for a meal and that they wouldn't be back until late. Julie liked Simon. He was Richard's younger brother but in many ways, he was the older one. He was more in tune with life than Richard was and never went off on tangents, or dreams. He seemed to know what to say and when to say it. Simon never interrupted people when they spoke, unlike Richard, who seemed to have an interrupter button on every conversation, always having to get in first or have the last comment. It was perhaps the most infuriating thing about her husband, but Julie had become accustomed to it.

She walked into the shower and turned the cold water on, it came as a shock, but it seemed to do the trick as she began to lose the wooziness that came with all the drink she had consumed. Slowly, her body grew accustomed to the cold and she could feel a tingle in her face, as if the colour had returned, she turned the hot tap on and began to relax in its warmth.

Richard was busy at the PC; all the images had downloaded, he started a new folder and moved them inside. One by one he opened the images, scanning each one, before closing it. The aerial shots had been a fantastic way to view the island and he was really delighted that Peter had taken the time to arrange it. Peter was a skilful pilot; Richard knew that from the first time he flew with him over the rocks where he had said his prayer to the Goddess. So, it was more than ironic that all these years later the memory was repeating itself again, with two of the same players.

But that wasn't the only reason that Peter and Richard got on, they shared a good deal together during their time away. Many a drink had been taken in the confines of Richard's tent and much camaraderie had been borne out of their conversations, and both wished they didn't have to talk about. It was this affinity to a fate that neither could predict that had kept them close in the Gulf, an affinity that now lasted long after the sands were clear of the evidence of any invasion. Richard had made good friends in the army, but none quite as good as Peter.

He scanned another couple of the images and moved onto number ninety-five. Not surprisingly, none of what he had seen through the lens had come out, as it had all been his imagination working overtime. But as he cleared the images of the Roman Villa at Curium, the first set of images that featured Aphrodite's Rock appeared. He opened the screen to view the images at 200% ratio.

The Rocks were certainly impressive; flying above them gave a total different perspective of their surroundings. The waters below were blue out at sea then changed to light green as they got nearer to the coast, coloured by the seaweed closer to shore which affected the hue. The sandy almost orange coloured tops of the first big rock, the one that everyone called Aphrodite's Rock, glistened as the sun flashed across it and formed a long thin shadow like a pointing needle. Richard moved to the next image, one of the smaller rocks, the second one. It sat in the water, embedded halfway in with the other half showing on the surface. The third rock was the smallest of all; at least it looked that way as the water covered it almost to the top. It was furthest from shore and consequently in deeper water, though the clarity didn't make it seem that deep. Richard clicked to the next set of images, the ones he had taken as they passed over the setting for the second time.

These looked different; the rocks were in the background. These were shots he had taken of the sea below the rocks, the ones that he had been able to shoot without any glare from the sun or the motion of the sea. The glass, almost mirror-like surface of the water, also showed something else below the surface. Richard eased the magnifying glass symbol over the shape in the water then blew the image up and up. He sat back in the chair bolt upright, just as if he had been smacked or slapped hard against the face, because his face smarted into a grimace, as if he had seen an apparition before a scream, and then it melted into a grin, a wide grin.

In an instant, he was sober again. 'Oh my God... Now I understand why! Richard spoke aloud. Unable to contain his excitement, he ran to the bathroom almost slipping over on the floor. 'Jules... Jules...'

Julie, startled by the interruption, instinctively grabbed the shower curtain, pulling it across her. 'What... What is it?'

'This, you've got to see this.'

'What is it, is it the kids?' Her maternal instinct kicked into the conversation.

'No, it's nothing like that... but you've got to see it.'

'You're frightening me, is it some lizard or cockroach... it's not a snake, is it?'

'No, no, it's on the PC.'

'Christ, Richard, you get me out of the shower to show me something on the PC?'

'Yes... it's incredible. Come and see.'

Wet, dripping, annoyed, and clothed only in a towel, Julie got out of the shower and followed Richard. 'What? Show me then.'

Richard proudly pointed to the screen, careful not to touch it. 'She's there...look.'

'Who? Who's there?' Julie stood looking at the computer bemused by the revelation.

'She is... Aphrodite. Look... she's under the water!'

'What are you talking about?'

'Right there, look in the water, there, see her?'

'See what... I can't see anything' Julie moved closer to the screen as if to appease her husband. 'What, that spot there?'

'No, not just that, follow the pen line. See in the water? It's the shape of a woman's body. Can't you see it?' Richard traced his pen off the screen but over the outline of the shape.

'Well, there is something there, but a body, no, I can't see that.'

'She's there under the water, the Goddess of Love in rock, preserved for all time… and I found her.'

'Yes, ok, very nice, you found her. Now where's the number of those nice people with the white coats.'

'Julie!' Richard wanted his wife to take a little more interest than her current look of indifference in his discovery. He emphasised his point again. 'Fuck it! I'm not mad… she is there. Look, can't you see her? Look again, please.'

Julie peered down at the screen, holding the towel tight in front of her.

'That's why it's called Aphrodite's Rock… I knew there was something more to it, than just three rocks in the sea. I could sense there was another reason, and I have found it.'

'Ok, you have found her, it, but we are on holiday. And Goddess or no Goddess she is not going to spoil it. So, switch off the PC and come to bed. You can have your own little love goddess if you like. Once you switch the PC off.' Julie's wicked smirk promised more and Richard was quick to follow.

He chased his wife around the room and into the bedroom, slamming the door, the image on the lit PC still displaying the image of Aphrodite's Rock.

The two lovers had enjoyed each other so much due to possibly the drink or the atmosphere or just the thought that it was just the two of them, that when they did eventually fall asleep, it was in each other's arms, just as they had done in their younger years when their passion for each other had been at its most potent, tonight it had returned.

Richard woke from his slumber, gently unwrapped himself from his wife and leaned over to the bedside table. The room began to shake. He knew Cyprus had earthquakes but this was so unexpected, the lights flashed in the room, the walls shuddered, and the door burst open. He moved to hug Julie, but the bed was empty. He reached out into the empty space clawing for her. As he did, a male figure ran into the room with blood streaming from a head wound. He pointed straight at Richard. The lights had dimmed and it was difficult to make out who the figure was, but Richard sensed that he had seen this image before. The figure drew closer and closer, the blood now drizzling the bedclothes. Richard tried to shout, to scream, to open his mouth but nothing came. He was powerless as the figure reached out his hand towards him. In the murky shadows, he tried to grab the stranger's hand.

'She's coming for you!' The words echoed around the room from the darkness.

Richard recognised the face and voice of Private Jones and screamed. 'NO, NO, NO.'

Julie pulled Richard from the bed and shook him.

His eyes rolled for a fraction of a second and then he heard her.

'Richard, Richard, wake up. Wake up.' Julie moved her hand across Richard's sweaty face and wiped the moisture away with her the palm before delving into the bedside table and picking up a batch of tissues. She took a couple and gently smoothed her husband's face. 'Jesus, Richard, you scared me.' She too was shaking.

'I'm sorry, I had a bad dream. That's all, just a bad dream, sorry.' Richard settled back down into the bed and rested his head against the pillow.

Julie looked thoughtfully at her husband before she too relaxed and lay back on her own pillow. 'Why, Richard, why now? You haven't had a dream like that in years, so why now?' She repeated herself.

'I don't know, but it could have been the helicopter ride. Maybe that brought it back, or maybe it is just being here.'

'Yes, so why did you pick Cyprus, if that is the case? Nightmares like this happen for a reason, whatever that might be. Did you bring your pills?'

'Yes, I'll take one now. Sorry, Jules, and let's try to go back to sleep, I will just get some water and take a pill, I am okay, really I am.'

Julie turned over and closed her eyes, not seeing Richard as he left the room and made for the bathroom.

Richard rummaged around in his toiletry bag and found the prescribed pills. He took one out, went to the kitchen, opened the fridge, grabbed a cold-water bottle and drank its contents, swallowing the pill at the same time. As he returned to the bedroom, he noticed the PC was still on. Placing one finger on the touchpad, the image of the goddess appeared. He smiled, his nightmarish visions had given way to something more tranquil, serene, and more mystical than he could have ever imagined. Once before, in the Gulf, she had been his sanctuary and escape from the nightmares. She was doing it again. A smile spread over his face at the realisation, as he shut down the laptop and returned to the bedroom.

Richard arose early. He was excited, too excited to sleep. He had tossed and turned throughout the night, but now he was on a mission, his adrenalin flowing faster than his thoughts.

Julie wandered out of the bedroom, to hear her husband on the cell phone.

'Is that for the day...or for the week? I see, ok... how much... umm, bit pricey... do you have any available today... yes, today? I can be there in an hour... just the one set... yes... thanks.'

Julie sat on the arm of the sofa and leaned over towards her husband. 'What are you up to now?'

'Jules, it's been playing on my mind all night... I just have to find out if she's there. Let me go there. Get it out of my system.'

'Go where? You just had a terrible nightmare and now you want to go somewhere, where? Oh no, not this Goddess thing again... this is really starting to piss me off now. What do you expect to find? She's not real. She is a bunch of rocks, in the water on the top, and now underneath, according to you!'

'I know... but I need to see for myself.'

'See what? I don't understand what you're trying to prove... Well, you can go on your own, the place gives me the creeps.'

'I'll be back soon, before dinner, promise. I just have to pick up some equipment'

'What?' Julie was becoming really annoyed and upset by the conversation.

'Diving equipment. I called the shop, they've got some.'

Julie stared at Richard, holding back the anger and the tears. 'Here we go again… how much is that going to cost, eh? Oh, shit, you go, Richard, just go, will you?'

Richard leaned over to kiss his wife and for the first time in days she ignored him and walked back to the bathroom. Richard shut the door loudly and started towards the car.

Julie shut the door behind her and found it hard to hold back the tears.

An hour and a half had gone by before Richard arrived at Aphrodite's Rock and there were only about a dozen tourists on the beach, but above him on the roadside, a coach had just stopped and was unloading its passengers. The guide was edging them towards the tourist shop and restaurant, from where he would get his usual commissions, introductions, and referrals.

The sun was hot on the shore and the water shimmered. Richard climbed into the wet suit he had hired, which was more to protect his skin from the tank on his back, but it was as Julie would have said an extra unnecessary expense. She was right too, because Richard didn't need any equipment at all. Fully kitted up, he waded out into the water and was able to still touch the bottom as he got to the second rock. The bottom shelved out slightly going down to about eight to ten feet, but it still wasn't deep. What was immediately noticeable was the strong tide and current as the wind created a vortex, which whipped the waves higher as they crashed against the rocks; it was a relentless movement of water against rock, timeless and perpetual.

Richard moved back to the second rock, the area he saw as the shape of the body lay just below the surface. He didn't need any equipment all he needed was the mask. He spat into the tube and ducked his head into the water. He saw the rocks totally indistinguishable from the image he had taken on the camera. Julie was right; there were no unique features to the shape. But he was taking it as matter of faith because somehow, he did feel something. There was something about the place, and he felt its presence. He dipped his hand below the water about a foot. Anyone could easily duck their head in and touch the rock. His mind and imagination suddenly kicked in as his hand stroked the smooth rocks below.

Julie had left the apartment and had walked the streets of the tourist area, stopping only for a coffee. She had bought some extra food items and was walking slowly back to the apartment when she saw the shop that sold all the Greek Mythology figures, she went inside. This time, she took a little longer to explore the place. She wandered up and down the aisles, looking at the various souvenirs and tourist tit-bits. The carousel in the centre of the store displayed a fine collection of postcards, some modern, some traditional, some crude. She twirled it around and saw a book on Aphrodite; a somewhat bigger version of a magazine. She opened it and flicked through the glossy pictures. Much of the imagery she had seen before, but there were also other pictures that she hadn't. Picking it up, she walked towards the counter to pay. As she queued, she saw the perfect present to give to her husband; she snatched it quickly and added it to the book.

Richard sat drying in the sun, his diving equipment neatly stacked beside him. He watched as the people came down the steps behind him and fanned out across the stones and shingle. Some tried to climb the first rock; others scaled it easily, without too much effort even though there was a sign saying *No Climbing* in Greek, English and Russian. All the people who came seemed curiously interested in the legend and the site itself, but there the activity seemed to end, for there was little else for them to do. It was after all just a spectacle. Once you had seen one rock, or in this case three, you had seen them all. Richard collected his things and slung the equipment into the holdall and trudged across the stones to the steps. He had much to think about as he opened the car door and started the engine.

It was quiet in the apartment; Julie sat reading the guide-book and making mental notes of where she would like to go next. The balcony chair was a great suntrap and already her face was turning from a bright red to a slightly tanned brown. She put some more suntan lotion on her face to trap the sun even more.

Richard swung the apartment door open and immediately saw his wife sitting on the balcony. His first movement was to go across and seek her forgiveness, but would she still be angry? He hoped she wasn't and that he could return to her good books.

'Did you find her?' Julie looked at him with a wry smile on her face.

'Well, in a funny kind of way I did.'

His reply caught her by surprise. 'Now what are you saying?' She queried.

'Do you have any idea how many people visit that place?' Richard was looking for a way to explain the thoughts that were buzzing around inside his head.

'Hundreds a year, maybe thousands,' Julie responded.

'And what do they do there, apart from take pictures and buy souvenirs?' Richard continued.

'Nothing, there's nothing else there, except the sea, from what I've read. And I don't suppose many go swimming, the current is too strong, so what else is there? There's nothing else beside the rocks.' Julie answered his question expertly.

'That's right, the rocks and a lot of cheap tourist tat in the shops.'

'Like this?' Julie handed Richard the small figurine of Aphrodite. 'I got it just in case you didn't find her, but it would appear you did.'

'Oh, thanks, she's great.' He held the figure in his hand. 'I know this will sound crazy to you Jules, but I have an idea, so just hear me out. What if we could make the Goddess and her legend, seem more real?' Richard used the figure as a visual aid to add weight to his proposal.

'How?' Julie was more than a little curious.

'By using the idea of the rocks below the water as a way of promoting the place. I've checked, the water is not deep, not from the shore to the second rock, only about four to five feet, and that's where she is. Well, the body shape is. So, if we were to run a rope from the shore to those rocks we could offer people the chance to submerge to kiss the Goddess, a sort of Cypriot Blarney Stone. We could make a fortune.'

'You're serious, aren't you?'

'Yes. I think it could be a good little business for us.'

Julie noticed the fire in his eyes and the way his mind was ticking and how he was making it all add up 'Do you realize what you're suggesting?'

'Yes, we move to Cyprus.' Richard announced and sat down.

Julie in contrast, stood to her feet, amazed at such a blatant suggestion.

CHAPTER SEVEN

THE PLAN

The sun had gone down and the moon was half full, it was a warm evening filled with the sound of traffic and cicadas which sounded like demented crickets that chorused between the spaces of when cars were and weren't passing them. Richard and Julie had not ventured far from the apartment, choosing to take their evening meal at the local Pizza Hut, not far from Dasoudi Beach.

As they sat at the table, Julie was not in a good mood, still trying to come to terms with the announcement Richard had made earlier about their impending move to Cyprus and what that could mean for her. She picked up her glass and took a long drink from the cold beer. 'WE can't just move like that, we have responsibilities. What about the kids?'

'We can bring them out here. Matthew is his own man now anyway and Molly's still at University and after that she wants to go around the world. What more can we do for them? Later, if it works out we can bring Molly out here if she wants to come; say as a starting point for her trip, that way we can keep an eye on her, at least for a while. Jules, look, we can try it for a year. Keep the house and rent it out. If it doesn't work we'll go back.' Richard's scheme seemed quite comprehensive.

'How long have you been planning this?' Julie remained unconvinced.

'I didn't plan anything; it just came to me as I sat on the beach today.'

'You're asking a lot, for just an idea, sacrificing your family like this...'

He wasn't sure but there appeared to be just a chink in Julie's armour of negativity.

'Besides, how do you think you can make any money doing this?'

'I don't know for sure. The place already attracts a big crowd, so offering something different we could do ok.'

Richard's argument was still not convincing enough but it did sound as if it could be done which was the frustrating part of it all. As if to lengthen her opposition Julie repeated the question. 'How are you going to make any money?'

'We charge for a dive, although, strictly speaking, it's not a dive, more a bob down in the water.'

'It won't work. You will need a licence and equipment.'

'A few masks possibly, but nothing else, oh, and a long rope. But you might be right about a licence, even though, strictly speaking,' he accentuated. 'It's not a dive.'

'I think it's crazy! I think you're crazy, and I think I'm crazier to even consider it. But, ok, say I agreed; how are you going to publicise this?'

'We will write to the local newspapers. Maybe Peter has some connections. He has been here a while and it's a small island.' Richard was buzzing again. 'You heard what he said today.'

'Yes, I think he is as crazy as you, but if it worked it could be good. It's certainly crazy enough to work.' Julie's

Bostonian speech was becoming more prominent with every sentence.

'So you're coming around to the idea?' Richard eased the question across to her.

'No, I haven't said that yet! I would need to see what sort of reaction you get first before I agree to anything.'

'That's fair, and I will find out about getting a licence. You're a good writer, put something together... then we send it in with a copy of the picture. How's that? If we don't get a response or reaction then it's finished, ok?'

'What about our holiday?'

The comment was apt under the circumstances and it was something Richard had not given a moment's thought to. 'If this works out; we could be on holiday, permanently. Cheers.' He raised his glass just as the waiter brought the large deep pan pizza to the table. It was just the distraction he needed to lighten the mood.

Earlier in the afternoon, Peter had arrived at the apartment. He had received Richard's intriguing text and become more than a little curious about the message. *Do you know anybody in the newspapers here?* It was the sort of message that demanded a concrete response, so he had driven over.

Peter sat drinking coffee, Julie sat close to the laptop going over the images, as the conversation, most of which was coming from Richard, grew in volume as a slightly bemused Peter sat on the sofa.

'Peter, I need your help, but first I need to show you something.' Richard had his full attention now as he began clicking the images on the screen. 'When we flew over Aphrodite's Rocks I took some shots on the second pass that have come back with something unusual, see what you make of it.'

Peter stood at the PC next to Richard.

Julie watched him as the screen produced an image first in normal view and then as Richard zoomed it to 200% she witnessed his reaction first-hand.

'Good God, what's that?'

'You see it?' Richard fired his question back at him.

'Yes, it looks like a shape in the water, a woman's body.'

'You see it that clearly?' Julie was amazed at the quickness of Peter's discovery.

'Yes, it's there in the water, the outline of a woman's body in the rocks.'

'Oh, great, Pete, I could kiss you... brilliant, he sees it. Julie, he sees it.'

'You really see it?' Julie doubted him again.

'Yes, I see these sorts of things easily. I don't know why, but maybe it's the training and the way we are taught to recognise shapes, so yes, I see that one. It's like the picture of Christ's face in the snow... some people don't see it, I saw it right away.'

'What picture?' Julie questioned him.

'It was taken by some Chinese guy in the 50's as he was climbing this mountain; he had a crisis of faith and some mysterious voice told him to take a picture of the scenery below. When he developed the picture, Christ's face was in the snow. They published it in the newspapers and I saw it right away. I see lots of those images. Remember the magic eye images? I used to get all of those. So yes, I see your woman in the rocks. Why?'

Richard looked straight at Peter. 'Because I think we can make that woman in the rocks come to life, with a bit of media attention and a bit of faith'. He had set his plan in motion and now Peter was in on it too.

That afternoon, it was not just the three of them who had been busy. Sheila had plans of her own and she had made sure that nobody was about to discover them. She had done her shopping list and got herself ready. Peter had told her he had a text from Richard and was going over to see him about it. It was just the sort of distraction Sheila needed; in fact, she couldn't have planned it better. It would give her a couple of hours at least for her own excursion.

She waited for Peter to leave before she went out to her car and drove off in the direction of Paphos. The roads were quiet as she passed the signpost to Aphrodite's Rock. 'What a place to come to on your first night.' She mused, as she accelerated past the sign.

She was in Paphos in less than half an hour and weaved her way through the one-way system to turn down a small beach road, near Kato Paphos, at the end of which was a large detached beach house, which overlooked the sea. She parked a short distance from the house, smoothed her dress down, checked her hair and make-up, and eased herself out of the car. She walked swiftly towards the large gate and pressed the buzzer, the gate swung open and she walked up the driveway to a large wooden door already opened.

A tall man stood at the door. He was Greek in appearance and characteristics, being well-tanned with neatly cropped hair, just a couple of cuts away from bald, wearing a black open-necked shirt, three buttons undone to reveal his hairy chest and sporting a pair of designer jeans with a thick black belt supporting them. At first glance his looks would place him in his thirties, but in reality, he was forty-five, at least.

Sheila walked up to him and kissed him passionately, he returned the gesture, pulling her inside the house and stripping the dress from her. He moved his hands over her body as he fondled her and lavished her with long lingering kisses; she grabbed at his jeans and unbuckled his belt. The passion intensified and it was not clear if they would make it to the bedroom or would just enjoy themselves as they stood pawing each other.

Sheila made her demands obvious. 'Fuck me now, Georgiou, I can't wait.'

Georgiou did as he was told.

Sheila had finished dressing and was tidying up her makeup and re-applying lipstick, as she sat on the side of the bed, when her lover crept closer and kissed the back of her neck. 'No, you will have to wait, I have to get back before Peter gets home. I do love it when you fuck me, but I have to go. But there will be more time; his friend is here so it gives me an excuse to go out more.'

'But, I want you now.' The man's hands moved to the front of her dress and moved inside.

'No, George, not now. Behave. Besides, how long are you going to keep me hanging on? I want to get out of that house and be with you but you keep telling me not yet.'

'I promise you it won't be too much longer. I have a big deal coming up with some Russians, once that is done you move in, okay?'

'Okay, but don't keep me waiting too long, naughty boy. Now I must go. I will text you.' She kissed him, leaving the faintest trace of her lipstick on his lips and the scent of her perfume on his face.

CHAPTER EIGHT

THE GODS ARE ON YOUR SIDE

The next morning, Peter and Richard set off on the motorway road to Paphos; they had to be there before twelve, as government offices usually close by that time. Careful to avoid the speed-traps that the police had set up, their drive was a mix of up and down on the accelerator. Even so, Peter's automatic was a smoother ride and much more comfortable than Richard's hire vehicle. They passed the Pissouri sign and headed on to Paphos. The tourist coaches that rattled passed heading either for the airport or for Petra Tou Romiou. The tell-tale indicator showed they were turning left to the Rocks. Peter accelerated past them towards Paphos.

Julie had almost come to terms with the idea Richard had proposed and now was seconded by Peter, feeling obligated to become part of the party. She scanned the pictures, opened a word document and typed in the title. IS THE GODDESS THERE?

Peter turned off the main Paphos Road and into a more suburban type district at the back of the seafront. The council building, he knew was sure to be busy with parked cars and finding a spot would not be easy. He opted to leave the car on the pavement, off the road, and out of sight of the police.

Richard had a few notes with him and a lot of hope in his pocket as they walked back towards the buildings.

Peter's expression was not as optimistic. 'Richard, this is going to take a long time. The wheels of commerce and councils grind slow here.'

'I thought they might. But I am just applying for a diving licence, that's all'.

'You're not telling them where and why?'

'Not now; just a quick application, keep it simple, eh?'

'I think it's a great idea, Rich but you've got to be careful, because once they find out what you're up to they will stop you and do it on their own.'

'Probably, but by then I hope the publicity wagon will be rolling.'

'It's a risky strategy.' Peter entered the building first and went over to the reception. He spoke a few words in Greek and the security guard pointed with his finger to the corridor on the left. As both walked over, they noticed a tall man standing at the water cooler.

He looked at Peter and then Richard.

'Signomi…' but before Peter finished the sentence the man returned his request.

'I speak English.'

'Good, my friend wants to get a diving licence. He is starting a diving school or thinking of it, what does he have to do?'

'Licences are on the third floor. You need to go there, but take the stairs, the lift doesn't work.'

Peter and Richard nodded their thanks. They strode up the stairs past the first floor then the second, until they arrived at the third. There were a number of men hanging about; all looked like agents with their clipboards; paid agents who took all the hassles out of applying for documents and licenses for people living on the island or hoping to; because in this world it was who you knew that got you the necessary documents, not what.

Peter recognised some of the paperwork on the clipboards; which seemed to be for driving licenses. Did the man downstairs miss-hear what he had asked him? He had clearly stated diving not driving. Peter became his own agent and walked over to a glass window, where a young Cypriot girl stared back at him, as she listened to his best Greek and responded by handing him an orange coloured form. Together, he and Richard filled in the form in Greek and English. Surprisingly, there wasn't a lot of information required, the usual questions and then a blank space to record your reason for the application.

Peter handed the form to the girl, who checked it then asked for a passport. Richard fumbled in his file and handed it to Peter. She stamped something on the form and asked for fifty Euros. Richard handed the notes to Peter. The girl stamped the form again and gave it back to him, the word APPROVED in Greek and English bold across the top. Peter wanted to ask if that was all they needed, but didn't, he simply took the form back and handed it to Richard. Equally stunned by the swiftness of such an operation, they picked themselves up and walked back down the stairs.

Peter turned to Richard and smiling made the most relevant comment he could make, 'I think the Gods are on your side. I have never seen anything like that before. Not out here.'

Richard surreptitiously uncrossed his fingers and his smile was total. 'Now let's go talk to Costa at the restaurant, I think he can help too.'

The two men had become like schoolboys, chatting and laughing, full of anticipation and excitement. For them, the adventure was just beginning. Peter started the car and pulled out sharply, a Greek man in an old beat-up Honda shouted through his window some obscenities as he braked hard, just as Peter's car sped away. More laughter accompanied the near miss.

Peter drove up the hill to the restaurant and noticed that there were only three cars in the parking area.

Richard clambered out and was first up the small set of steps and into the restaurant.

Peter shut the door, and instinctively locked it. Habits of the old country still not easy to shake, although most Cypriots left their cars unlocked.

Costa sat at the bar in the corner of the restaurant, pouring over the Greek news. He recognised Richard almost immediately and stood up to offer his hand, his smile broad and welcoming. 'Hello, good to see you again, how are you enjoying your holiday?'

'Great, thanks, this is my friend Peter.'

'Nice to meet you.'

'I've eaten here a few times in the past, but we have never actually met as such.'

'Yes, I think I've seen you here once or twice, you live near here?'

'Pissouri.'

'Oh, local then. Anyway, coffee or beer, gents? What can I get for you?'

'We will have two beers, please, and I want to ask you a question.' Richard gets up off the stool at the bar and looks at Costa, his face quite serious.

'Two beers it is. So, what is the question?' Costa opens the beer bottles and hands them over.

'Costa, do you believe in Jesus?'

Costa's face registered surprise and he was not just a little taken back by the question. 'What do you take me for, this is an orthodox country and I'm orthodox.'

'Good because I've got something to show you.' Richard leaned down to pick up his laptop case.

Julie had finished the piece. She was a good writer as Richard had said; a skill she had developed over the years. She would like to have been a writer but somehow life had simply gotten in the way, besides, she would never have had the patience to write a book. But perhaps if they did settle in Cyprus she would have the time.

She had used the pictures effectively in the copy and had also referred to the story Peter had mentioned about Christ's image in the snow. She also tied in faith into the article, saying that faith was a matter of personal belief; you either were a believer or you weren't, you either saw the image in the sea or you didn't. It was that simple. Julie read it over and over, looking for any grammar or spelling mistakes, there weren't any, something she had also perfected, the art of writing correctly. All too often Julie would read something that she saw as written badly and would like to correct, but didn't, instead, she stopped reading it. She was no critic, she just knew what she liked.

Richard and Peter came through the door almost together; there was no containing Richard's excitement or indeed Peter's enthusiasm. Both were on a roll.

'We got it.' Richard waved the orange paper in front of Julie and then handed it to her.

'Julie, I have never seen anything like it. Over here that's classed as a miracle, there's so much red tape on this island.' Peter's confirmation of the minor wonder seemed to add credence to the surreal event.

'Anyway, we got it. How are you getting on?' Richard asked his wife.

'It's done, it's called; Is the goddess there?'

'Great title, Jules, and we have the pictures to back it up. We'll send it off to the papers. You said you knew someone, Pete?'

'Yes, there are a couple of papers. Cyprus Weekly, Cyprus Mail and then there's the Cyprus Lion, that's the Forces' paper. Oh, and there are all the Greek papers.'

'Well, I have only written it in English, so we will only send it to them then maybe the Greeks will pick it up.' Julie sat back, pleased with her work; she hoped the papers would be too.

'They usually do if the stories are interesting enough.' Peter was also keen to get the story circulated. 'I will send it to a couple of people I know.'

'Now all I need is a long rope.' Richard broke the conversation down by changing the subject and looked around the room as if he was searching for one.

'I think I know where you can find one of those. You need a fisherman's rope and I have one. Oh, didn't I tell you, I own a boat as well.' Peter grinned.

'No you didn't!' Richard's somewhat surprised expression sparked laughter.

It was left to Julie to finish the sentence and the sentiment. 'Now after this; can I start my holiday?'

CHAPTER NINE

IT BEGINS

The next two days were spent as they should have been when one is on holiday, relaxing in the sun, swimming in the warm waters and soaking up the atmosphere. And interspersed with these cool and 'chilling' exercises were the off-beach excursions to tourist sites.

Curium was their chosen base point as it offered the best of both worlds; it was also easy to get to, and the beaches though not golden, were sandy and there was little in the way of stones or rocks underfoot once you were in the sea. The waters were also not deep; wading into them was easy until the temptation to give way to a dive into the breakers became irresistible. Richard was a good swimmer both on and under water, his army training had gotten him his qualification for scuba diving training and he had always felt comfortable in the sea.

Julie usually preferred the safety and comfort of a concrete pool but at Curium, she took to the water without hesitation. As she moved through the waters, her tan was becoming noticeable against the white lines of her pink bikini. Her figure had remained good all these years and her body showed little signs of her age, there were no sagging pieces or cellulite, as she had tried to keep herself in good shape. She did a lot of walking back home and that seemed to keep her fit, that and the odd trip to the gym. The quick glances from some of other men in and around the beach told their own story; Julie was a good-looking woman.

Richard dived into the water through the crashing white foam that enveloped him and then spat him out. His body felt exhilarated by the force of the waves as they swept over him, and felt the cold chill for just an instant as the waves covered him only to disappear upon the shore. Julie joined him; they were alone for the first time in a while. Yes, they had been together; but not as a couple, there had been too many other matters that took their personal attention and pulled them away from each other. But in the waves, *one on one,* they were together. The water pounded them for a few seconds and then subsided and turned to a slow undulation. The tension that had been building between them subsided; a feeling of contentment coming over them as they stood looking out to sea and the sun made their skin bristle and burn.

'Hungry?' Richard's one perceptive word was enough to move them back to the shore.

Julie held her husband's hand and they walked together through the waves to towel themselves dry and collect their things.

The restaurant was just fifty yards away and they chose one of the tables closest to the shore. It was a busy day and there was a mix of staff; some Russian, others European, and some Cypriot. A mixed bag of food was on offer, from traditional Greek style dishes to the fast food western alternatives of hamburgers and chips and of course fish in all different shapes and sizes, including shellfish and lobsters; everything for the tourist and their appetites.

Richard chose a mixed kebab whilst Julie tucked into some pasta, they drank cold beer and smiled and laughed a lot. There was a closeness about them again, and an understanding of each other's needs. Until the cell phone rang.

The three-ring tones punctured the moment, as Richard didn't recognize the number but answered the call anyway. 'Hello... Hi, yes... speaking... oh, thank you.' He mouthed across to Julie. 'It's in the Paper,' then returned to the call. 'That's great. Yes... thank you.' He hung up and leaned over to kiss Julie. His eyes and body already returned to the excited state of days before. 'They're going to run it tomorrow.' He punched in another number and without further reference to Julie greeted Peter. 'Hello, Pete. Guess what, I am going to need your rope. Yes, yes, do that, great, we will see you back there then, ok, fine, bye'. He hung up the cell phone and stood up; he walked over to the waiter to get the bill ordered quickly.

Julie finished the last of her beer and sat back in the chair thinking 'Well, that's the holiday over.'

By two thirty, Richard and Julie were back at the apartment He unloaded the beach bags and towels from the car, while inside, Julie had opened the balcony door and was placing the towels on the railing to dry. The heat of the balcony was intense and acted as a sun trap. Julie moved into the shade, to protect herself from the heat.

A small truck pulled into the apartment drive. It was Peter.

Richard came across to him.

'I borrowed this to bring the stuff in.' Peter pulled down the back of the truck. Inside were two five-foot poles and a coiled rope. 'I got these off a mate I know, who uses it for his fencing, so it should do the trick.'

Richard held one of the poles in his hand and gripped it firmly. The steel was strong, that was for sure and the pole had a curve at the top like a shepherd's crook where the rope could be tied around. Richard felt delighted with this and thanked his friend. 'These are great, just great, we can wrap the rope around this bit and then secure it. Hopefully, the rope will stretch all the way to the water's edge, it's just a case of making it secure. I don't suppose I can borrow your toolbox?'

Peter returned the smile and handed him a large blue metal toolbox that contained a variety of tools.

Richard searched the box, what he needed most of all was a heavy hammer; he found that at the bottom.

'It looks like you're all set.' Peter said.

'It does. I think I will be able to squeeze those poles into the car. I don't suppose you fancy a ride down to the rocks to try it out, do you?'

'How else are you going to get this done?' Peter chided him pointing to the truck.

Julie came out to see the two men chatting, she watched them as they picked up the poles and rope and put them back into the truck. She knew exactly what to expect next.

'Jules, we are going to try this out, see if it works, ok?'

Before Julie could respond, Richard had climbed into the truck's cab and the engine started. She just waved her acceptance as the truck pulled away. Returning to the apartment, the balcony looked like an inviting place to sunbathe. She laid the towel down on the floor and placed a couple of thick towels on top of it to rest her head against, after which she smothered herself with suntan lotion, letting the sticky substance evaporated into her skin. She removed her bra and covered her breasts with lotion and lay down on the towel to bathe in the sun.

The truck couldn't get down to the beach, so they parked on the roadside above; they clambered out, taking the poles and ropes from the back. There were only a couple of people on the shore; it was as if people came to the site in dribs and drabs.

Richard crunched across the stones, eager to try his experiment. He waded into the water, his shorts still dry by the time he reached the edge of the second rock. He saw a rock below the surface that appeared to have a natural ledge to it. He pushed the first pole into the sand below and wedged one of the submerged rocks against it then moved another to wedge it against the other side of the pole. He then placed the coiled rope around the top and made a Sheepshank knot in the metal.

Army training came in handy even in the most unusual circumstances, such as this; he fed the other part of the rope back towards Peter. There was a sagging section to the rope but once it was secure he positioned the pole again in the sand and supported with more rocks. The rope tightened and became straight, and a third pole in the middle of the other two would make the thing that much more secure, but for now, all Richard needed to know was; did it work? With the two poles in place, he started back down the rope to the second rock then paused; the water was colder now even though the sun was shining directly on it. 'Here goes!' he shouted back to Peter and dipped his head below the water. His face touched the rocks below. It worked.

Richard and Julie finished supper, Peter had left them earlier and it was just the two of them in the apartment. The sun had gone down over an hour ago and the warm night air wafted from the sea towards the balcony. Julie had taken up her favourite place, seated at the balcony table overlooking the pool.

Richard had finished clearing the dishes and was just making coffee. 'Jules, I am going to get up early tomorrow, just in case anybody shows up. You have a lie in, hon.'

The conciliatory offer was lost on Julie. Still, there was no dampening his enthusiasm; he was so hyped up, thinking that his idea could come to fruition. 'Fine; I am going to go sunbathing on the beach out there; I've picked out my spot already.' Julie pointed to an unseen spot ahead of her.

Richard moved to the back of the cupboard where the suitcases were and pulled out something. 'We made this earlier. What do you think?'

It was a large bed sheet that had written across it in English and Greek DIVE TO SEE THE GODDESS. ONLY £4.00.

Julie's pragmatic expression seemed to sum it all up, 'Richard, I really hope this is worth all the trouble.' Then as if to really nail him down she delivered the question that he knew would eventually come. 'So, tell me exactly why you are doing this? Why we are giving up our holiday, one we have saved for a long time to have; because we have not had one alone ever since the kids were born. Why are we giving it all up so you can go play explorers at a bloody tourist site? Tell me what's so special about Aphrodite's Rock?' The twang was back with a vengeance.

Richard sat at the table facing her. then looked into her eyes as if he was confessing an untruth. 'I have been to Aphrodite's Rock before, before we drove there from the airport; well, at least I had seen it. That is, from the road, while in a truck on the way to the Gulf in '91 and then again on the chopper going out to sea to pick up the ship. On that chopper, I was so scared of what might happen I prayed to her; prayed to the Goddess to bring me home to you. It's stupid I know, pure impulse it was, anyway, as I said my little prayer, this beam of moonlight came from the rocks. I took it as a sort of acknowledgement that she had heard me.'

'Christ all mighty, Richard!' Julie couldn't comprehend what she was hearing.

Richard continued. 'Then just before we were ready to go to war I kept myself occupied reading about the place and her legends. I don't know but somehow it kept my mind off the war and what lay ahead. So maybe because of that I owe her something, and maybe by discovering the body in the rocks, more people will visit the site. I think that's the point, she wants more people to come and see her.'

'She...' Julie's expression was one of incredulity. 'I don't understand this, Richard, not at all; it's as if you planned it, before we even arrived. Did you know anything about the figure in the rocks before we got here?'

'No Jules, I swear I didn't, it was a pure fluke that I discovered it.'

'Sometimes Richard you are quite mad! And this is one of those times. But you have made me a part of it anyway, so I will play along. But I warn you, don't get obsessed with this idea. There's only one woman in your life and I am not about to share you with anybody else, flesh or myth.' Julie reached over and drank her coffee slowly; she had made her point succinctly.

CHAPTER TEN

YOU WILL NOT BELIEVE THIS

As promised, Richard let Julie sleep in.

Or so she thought, because she was rudely awakened by her cell phone ringing. She had only used it once before since she had been here and that was to talk to Molly, so she instinctively got up thinking the call was from one of her children.

There was a great deal of background noise so she couldn't hear very well as the signal kept dipping in and out. 'Hello.' she shouted again.

'Hello' Richard was on the phone, excited and breathless, almost speechless. The cell spluttered out his words. 'Jules…Jules…you won't believe this… I don't. You've got to see this, Jules, there's so many… you got to… please come now… ask Peter to bring you, please…. I need you!'

'Richard… Richard.' Julie tried to get him back, but his cell was dead. Julie began to look for Peter's number on the notepad and called it quickly. 'Peter, sorry. Can you help me? I think Richard's in trouble at Aphrodite's Rock… can you take me there? Thanks.'

Peter was in town, so he was able to get to Julie within ten minutes. Julie climbed into the car and the automatic sped towards the motorway, reaching it within five minutes and then speeding towards Paphos. The traffic was getting busier and busier and with every mile the number of cars got larger and larger. As they passed Episkopi the accelerator was almost flat to the floor as Peter rushed past the slower cars, but then he had to slow dramatically and brake hard as there was a traffic jam ahead. He couldn't see what the hold-up was and wondered if it might be an accident, as Cyprus roads were notorious for this, but neither could he see any police vehicles or ambulances. The traffic moved slowly as they approached a large column of vans, several of which looked like mobile broadcasting units, with an array of satellite equipment on their roofs.

Further on there were a number of smaller four-wheel drive cars that carried big 'Press' badges on the front of their windscreen. Peter took a quick glance at them and pulled the car across ahead of the column. The road forward was clearer, and he took a shortcut through one of the turnings, which brought him along the coast road towards Petra Tou Romiou. The road was crammed with cars parked on the roadside and people walked in one direction. There were a couple of police cars parked with their blue lights flashing on and off, but no officers visible. The atmosphere seemed quite relaxed, for such a large crowd, and there was no panic.

As they got closer to the inner road, Peter stopped the car, he couldn't drive any further. 'We'll walk from here.'

Julie acknowledged him and they both got out.

They hurried past a group of people, who looked like tourists and in front of them there was a small group gathered around a TV crew. There was a young Greek Woman speaking to camera, ahead of her was another crew, with the usual bank of microphones, from ERT, Rick, Capital, and Mega, all vying to grab the attention of the speaker. The crowds moved slowly forward.

Seeing a gap, Peter began to climb down the cliff side, while holding Julie's hand to steady her as they made their way down the slope to the beach. As they reached the shore, they looked back up to see several others now following in their footsteps. A multitude had swollen the shoreline. Slowly, they picked their way over to the area where most of the people were standing reaching the rock, which had the largest gathering, there were a number of 'Vox Pops' taking place on the beach at every few feet.

Through the melee, Julie saw Richard. He was holding his rope in his hands and guiding people along. Peter and Julie pushed their way past the crowds to reach him.

There was no disguising Richard's delight. 'See, I told you she was here and all these people want to see her.' He couldn't contain his excitement or his laughter.

Peter summed it all up in one expression. 'You're gonna need a bigger rope!'

Richard hugged Julie and Peter and then barked out his instructions for them to try to get people in line.

The crowd grew larger as the throngs moved across the beach.

Still laughing, Richard guided the next lot of people on the rope.

Julie shuffled more people into line and then with Peter's help, things started to get into some order. 'I don't believe this... I just don't believe it.' Julie kept repeating the same phrase over and over again.

Some of the news people tried to get hold of Richard to interview, but he was immersed in water, people on the rope, and just too busy to talk to anyone.

The journalist then targeted Julie for a comment.

'I just don't believe any of this.'

A young suited Greek news reporter approached Julie, pushing a microphone towards her. 'Mrs. Cole, as Richard's wife, were you aware of your husband's discovery and were you a part of it?'

'Yes, I was aware, and I did help write the press release but I don't believe this.'

The Greek journalist, continued in English. 'And what do you think now, Mrs. Cole, do you think these rocks are really the body of the Goddess Aphrodite?'

'I don't know, I think you believe what you believe, it's a matter of faith, isn't it?' Julie's last composed comment brought the interview to a conclusion.

The reporter turned to camera. 'And so the legend lives on or so it would seem, at the site of the Goddess, where once again, Aphrodite has possibly risen from the sea.' The journalist nodded her thanks, the camera cut, and the crew moved over to another crowd of people.

And still the crowds continued to swarm onto the shore.

By the time they arrived back at their apartment, the events of the day had exhausted them. They were resting on the bed motionless; Richard had switched his mobile off, but Julie kept hers on.

Molly had seen her on TV and so had Matthew. They had no idea what was going on when their Mother appeared on the news at 1pm, again at 5pm, and then 7pm, in fact, throughout the day, the story that grabbed everyone's attention was the discovery of the body in rock. Julie assured them that she would explain everything when she got home.

Julie sat on the bed, as Richard opened a plastic bag. Inside were hundreds of notes; he also emptied his pockets and more spilled onto the covers. She began to count...

Richard stood watching her, her eyes were bright with excitement.

She stacked them into wads of one hundred and after she finished there were four piles in various denominations. 'There's almost eight hundred Euros here; that's two hundred people today.' She pointed to the pile of money.

'I know Jules. It would have been more but the sea got rough and it was difficult to take them out then. But tomorrow I will get another rope.'

'You're going back?'

'Of course. I started something, I am not about to let it go.'

'What about our holiday?'

'I told you if this kicks off we will be on permanent holiday.'

'I know, but what if I don't want to live here. Have you thought about that?'

'No. You do, don't you?'

'I don't know. I'm not sure.'

'Would you leave me here on my own?'

'Would you stay?'

'Yes, I think this is a real chance for us. I think this could be the one thing where we can finally get something good out of.'

'For you, you mean! Where do we come into it? Where do I come into it? What about work, have you thought of that? You can't just not show up. Besides, how are you going to make a living?'

Richard looked at his wife and the money on the bed: he tried to lighten the mood. 'Well, I'd say that's not a bad start.' He offered her a pile. 'I would concentrate on this. Besides, it looks like you're going to become the banker. Go on, count it again.'

'Yes, ok, you may well be able to make a go of it, but there's something here that needs to be said.' Julie looked straight at him.

He returned her look.

'Do you love me Richard?'

'Of course I do. You know that.'

'No, Richard, I mean... do you love me, not Julie the wife or Julie the Mother, or Julie the homemaker. Do you love me, me, Julie? Not what I am, but who I am. Do you love me?'

Richard didn't know what to say. He had paid lip service to her request but this was an answer he had to be careful about. This required the right words, not ones she expected to hear, but the ones she did not. 'Yes, I love you. Not because of what you are, or your abilities as a mother or a wife or a lover, I love you because you make me a better person, a whole person. Life would be a journey without direction, unless you are with me. You give me the strength to live it, to experience first-hand what love is through your eyes. I knew it the first night we were together that you were the only woman I would ever love like that; that you would always be my one true love. And no matter what tests come along I will stay with you. Yes, Julie, I love you. Is that what you wanted to hear? And if it means that much to know you,

I will give this idea up and come back home with you, now, today!'

Julie held him in her arms, crying a little, as she had never heard him speak to her like that before. And for once, she felt he meant every word because it was not what she expected to hear.

He hugged her, holding her tight.

Julie wiped the tears from her eyes. 'No, I don't want you to give up on your dream, and if you think you can make a go of it, then you do it. But I will need to go home to sort things out before I come out here, ok?'

The last sentence was all the proof that Richard needed, he had finally persuaded his wife to try a new life in Cyprus.

Julie held the money in her hand.

Richard gave her another pile.

'Just in one day?' She queried, the figures starting to add up in her head.

'Yes, and with a bigger rope we can take many more people, go on, count it again.'

CHAPTER ELEVEN

THE MiSTRESS OF THE ROCK

Richard had set the alarm for 6:30am. He wanted to be at the rocks early to get set up for the expected crowds. It was Sunday and the first tolls of the church bells rang out from across the road. He had left Julie sleeping, with last night's conversation fresh in his mind. So it wasn't only the clanging making his head ring this morning. He started the car, drove off towards the highway, and passed several people on their way to Church.

The orthodox religion was a powerful influence on the island; most people went to church weekly or on more than one occasion, unlike the so-called Christian worshippers at home. He drove carefully along the roads then picked up speed as he made his way along the inner carriageway before accelerating out onto the highway. The rope and poles were secure in the back of the car, the poles sticking through the sunroof opening; the breeze coming through was not welcome at this time of the day, but later it would be. The drive to the rocks was quick as there was little traffic at this time of the morning, reaching the turning within forty minutes of leaving Limassol.

He pulled off left and could just discern the outline of the beach as he made his way down the hill. At the bottom, he

115

turned right as it was a mere quarter of a mile from the site when he saw the road ahead as CLOSED. A large red sign in Greek and English stood in front of the coastal road leading to the site, with a police car parked behind it. There was no way to get through.

Richard pulled his car over to the side of the road and parked; then leaving the stuff in the car, he walked towards the policeman. Approaching the barrier, he asked the Policeman what was going on.

The officer ignored him.

Richard tried to pass by him, but from behind the car, a large Greek Man, heavy set and sporting an impressive black and grey beard and bright blue eyes, immaculately dressed in a black suit and an open necked shirt, and shiny black shoes walked towards them.

'I see your little publicity stunt has created quite a stir, Mr. Cole.' The Greek man spoke with a good command of English but with a strong Greek accent.

'Sorry?'

'I am Mr. Lukas Christoulides.' The man spoke with some authority. 'It was my department that gave you your licence. Walk with me, Mr. Cole.'

Richard knew this was not a request but an order.

Mr. Christoulides passed the barrier and moved out, crossing the road, Richard dutifully followed; the police officer seemed to ignore them both as they walked towards the edge overlooking the rocks. Lukas turned and spoke to Richard. 'But you weren't very honest with us, Mr. Cole, were you? You didn't tell us you were going to turn this revered site into a circus.'

'I didn't know this would happen.' Richard tried to argue back.

'No, I don't think anybody did, Mr. Cole. But, it has, and we face a dilemma, don't we, Mr. Cole?' The Greek's manner was one of a school master reprimanding a naughty pupil.

'Why?' Richard tried to play dumb.

'Because Mr. Cole, this is a site that has been here for over five thousand years, maybe longer.' He reached his arm outwards to prove the power of the attraction. 'So, we cannot afford to keep it closed for long. The restaurants and shops would complain, the hoteliers would complain. People would complain; we would lose face, Mr. Cole.'

'What exactly are you proposing then, that you take it over?'

'No, Mr. Cole, if we did that you would go running to the papers saying we used bully tactics to shut you down. Our credibility would be gone and we would lose face.'

'What then?' Richard had put the ball in Mr. Lukas' court.

'We will help you and in turn you will help us. Tomorrow, the beach will re-open, we will have a sectioned off fence and a path cleared through to the rocks; you will organize the dives as you call them and we will supply you with a full licence, insurance and bigger ropes to run your dives with. In return, half of what you make will be given to the community. Is that clear, Mr. Cole?'

'Yes, perfectly clear.' Richard knew then, it was Game, Set, and Match to Mr. Lukas.

'Oh, you will also need an alien permit as this will be a form of employment. Do you understand?'

'Yes I do, thank you.' Richard knew when he was truly beaten.

'Go back to your apartment, Mr. Cole. It is Sunday there will be no visitors today. An announcement has already been made that the site will remain closed for safety reasons, but tomorrow Mr. Cole, we will re-open Aphrodite's Rock.' Mr. Lukas offered his hand to Richard who took it and returned the gesture.

By the time Richard returned to his car and started back, the news had already been broadcasted that the site had closed, as several vehicles were doing about turns and heading back in the opposite direction. Mr. Lukas had some influence that was for sure and Richard felt that he had been lucky, very lucky indeed.

Peter and Sheila were already at the apartment. Their offering of Greek cakes and biscuits was more than welcome and Julie was munching on one of the crunchier varieties whilst Peter sank his teeth into one of the delicate cream fancy cakes.

Sheila ignored their offers and just drank her coffee, but though she may have lost her appetite there was no sign of her enthusiasm diminishing. She seemed to gobble up all the news items at once. 'It has been on BBC, CNN and Sky News all day and yesterday. They even showed the helicopter that Peter flew you in over the rocks.'

'Well, I hope they don't show that too often, it could get me into a bother if they keep at it. I don't think my boss encourages joy rides.'

'I hope it won't come to that.' Julie was genuinely worried by Peter's comment.

Sheila continued on her delivery of the newscasts. 'They have professors, archaeologists and sub-mariners discussing the bloody thing. They say the tourist office is overrun with requests from people all over the world; they are flying out in their droves to get here, hundreds, possibly thousands.'

'What have we started?' Julie used the 'we' word for the first time.

On queue Richard entered the apartment.

Julie walked across to him. 'Are you okay? We heard on the news that the site was closed today.'

'I'm fine, they're closing it to make it better, and that's what they're doing now. The people were there from the council and they said we could carry on, as long as we give them half the proceeds.'

'Bloody corruption is rife in this country.' Peter's acid comment was delivered as if he knew this was how things worked.

'Look, I don't mind. It was that or they would have shut me down and done it themselves. At least this way we get to stay open and we get half of what we make.' Richard had come to terms with the offer.

Sheila pointed to the TV screen. 'That could be a lot too; this is a scene from Larnaca airport this morning, just look at the crowds.'

'Oh Richard, what have you done?' Julie took another nibble from her crunchy biscuit and sank back onto the sofa watching the broadcast.

'I don't know, but one thing's for certain, I won't be going home for a while. Is there anymore coffee?' Richard sat back on the sofa with Julie as the four of them continued watching the TV. It was odd seeing someone, who was also in the same room as you on the screen. Perhaps this was something that all had to get used to from now on.

For the rest of the day, they sat by the pool trying to avoid pointing fingers, wandering eyes, and the requests from news and the media for more interviews. Peter acted as a sort of go-between for Richard and Julie, filtering journalists through for them and choosing whom they should speak to. A number of photographers gathered and their endless clicking got on everybody's nerves.

Richard wondered if this was what every day was going to be like henceforth, surely the novelty would wear off and another newsworthy story would hit the headlines? Still, it made a change from the horror and devastation of the crisis countries like Iraq and Afghanistan, conflicts that he had long put to bed in his mind, but were now being slowly resurrected in his dreams.

Eventually, even the media had to eat and the short respite gave them the opportunity to get out of the apartment and take a drive. They didn't turn towards the beach; instead, they headed for one of the small villages outside of Limassol. One village in particular was Julie's choice, Kalo Chorio; meaning 'Good Village' in Greek. Here, they produced the desert wine they had sampled on their trips around town, which already seemed a long time ago. Commandaria is the region where the desert wine is produced and Julie felt that the place might be the distraction they needed. It took only half an hour to reach the village on a Sunday as the roads were practically deserted; only one or two cars passed them in either direction as they wound their way around the hillside roads, ascending with every mile.

Kalo Chorio was a typical Cypriot hamlet, with typical Cypriot buildings, some traditional some more modern. It was popular with Brits, who wanted the peace and serenity which they found there. It also had a thriving local industry producing not only the famous Commandaria wine but also Olive Oil, which they farmed and harvested from the local Olive groves.

As they walked around, there was an array of fruit trees overshadowing the buildings or growing in some of the open fields and allotments: oranges, lemons, mandarins, including a mango tree and other Mediterranean fruits and varieties that they did not recognise scattered about the locale. They even spied the inconspicuous Gecko or village lizard scurrying between the houses.

The dried-up water tank, next to the AEOKA monument, a memorial to conflicts past with the British, made a good rendezvous point for visitors. But the main attraction was the winery from where the Commandaria was pressed. Entering the stone building, they moved from one century into the next, as decorating the walls were the people of the village; portraits in sepia-framed photographs and paintings. Spanning the generations, right through to the villagers of today, consecrated in pictures and held in esteem and reverence for all who visited. But this was really the only concession to the past and the present, because the huge silver-coated vats were futuristic-looking, with the plant having its own automated system. The ways of the old, had given way to progress.

Julie thanked the guide and walked hand in hand with Richard back to Peter's car; they all stopped for a drink at the *Taverna* and then paid their respects to the small church adjoining it. The icons inside were beautiful and Julie lit a candle, more in thanks than anything else. Peter and Richard waited outside, as the two women took time to pray silently.

'Let's go now, shall we?' Richard seemed eager to leave, he had other things on his mind and this was not the place for those sorts of thoughts.

'Why don't you come back with us tonight? There's plenty of room' Sheila offered.

'It's a lovely idea, but not tonight, Sheila. I know we haven't done a lot but I feel quite tired, must be this village air, it's so clean and clear.' Julie nodded her appreciation.

'And it's cool too, so cool.' Peter repeated himself, as he collected his thoughts as they all walked back to the car. 'Ok then, let's go.' Peter said and started the car.

By the time they were outside the apartment it was late. They had not intended to stop on the way back, but the restaurant off the road looked too good to turn down, and the meal lived up to all their expectations.

Julie suppressed a yawn, reminding everyone it was past all their bedtimes.

They said their goodnights and Peter and Sheila drove back to Pissouri.

Julie shut the door and hugged Richard. 'Thank you.'

'What for?' He looked puzzled.

'For taking me away for a few hours from the new you, back to the old you, that's what for.'

Richard held her in his arms, as he looked at her closely and spoke with feeling in his voice and from his heart. 'Jules, I'm sorry, I never meant for this to happen. I have really messed up your holiday, haven't I?'

'Uh Huh,' she smiled. 'But some dreams are worth following.' She smiled again, somehow conveying the message that all was okay.

'Julie Cole, I love you so much.' Richard kissed his wife. It was a deep passionate kiss that required no words, or gestures, nothing, just his lips on hers.

The alarm on the phone started first, then the beep, beep, beep of the alarm clock confirmed the time as six o'clock. Richard got up quickly and shaved almost at the same speed; he clambered into his shorts and a tee-shirt with open sleeves and put his sandals on.

Julie stirred and woke herself; she needed to see him leave, so she forced herself out.

He had got himself ready in just ten minutes, a record. With sleep gone and his night dreams faded, he was off to fulfil his day-dream.

Julie waved as she saw him disappear out the door and into the car. She waved again, knowing he couldn't see her but hoped he would, just not the tear that ran down her face.

Monday morning traffic was already building and the cars jockeyed for places in the lanes leading up to the highway, no one giving way as Richard edged his way out onto the main road. That was until a Keo lorry headed towards him and stamped on its brakes sharply, allowing Richard the space to get out. He accelerated sharply, his little hired car working overtime. It wasn't meant to do all these journeys, only supposed to be used for short trips to the beach and the occasional excursion. But presently, it was in full employment. Richard hoped it would not break down. He moved from third gear through to fourth and into fifth and was away.

Daybreak at the rocks was always a different experience as no two days were ever the same. The sun cast a multitude of endlessly-changing shadows and the tide never stayed constant across the shore. It was a performance that altered with every new day and audience. Already, several people were on the beach waiting and watching the water as it crashed onto the rocks. Mysticism was indelibly inscribed throughout the landscape. This was a setting for the great philosophers to ponder and pontificate and for the priests and priestesses to perform their rituals, or for men of wisdom to gather and deliver their pearls. History, myth, and magic mixed, into one place at Aphrodite's Rock. And now he, Richard, in his own small way was a part of that. It was a very thought-provoking idea.

Richard passed several more cars and coaches, signalling that he was about to turn left and the familiar signpost of Petra Tou Romiou welcomed him. A quarter of a mile away, the first visitors to the site were disembarking from their cars and coaches, the restaurants were busy with people sipping their morning coffee and teas. Their trade had never been so good. Richard parked in the restaurant space that had been reserved for him. He collected his equipment and made his way across to the beach steps. Several people recognized him and smiled and some followed. As he emerged on the shore, he immediately noticed the new set up.

Mr. Lukas had been true to his word, the beach could re-open and it would be better. Richard could clearly see a series of metallic poles in the water, positioned like a corral with a rope linked to the poles so that one could start at one end and follow it through to come out at the other. It looked neat and effective. There was also a clear pathway out to the rocks, no awkward large boulders or stones to negotiate, just a straight path. Only the waves were still as dominant as they had been before, but with the larger stones gone they now offered little resistance to people who waded out to the second rock, where the figure was. A line of people was waiting behind a sort of makeshift gate made of fencing,

He dropped his poles and rope, they were superfluous now. Richard stared around him, he appeared stunned by the change to the place.

'A beautiful day, Mr. Cole, you are going to be very busy, I can see. I suggest you get started, Mr. Cole.' Mr. Lukas stood looking out at the rocks and then gazed at Richard.

'Thank you. You did all this?'

Lukas ignored Richard's question as he handed him an envelope and grinned. 'Mr. Cole, you will need this.'

'What is it?'

'It is your alien card and work permit.'

'But I thought this would take months to get.'

Lukas smiled a knowing smile that said Richard knew nothing about the politics of the situation. 'I am sending some help over to you, Mr. Cole. They will be here soon, to keep an eye on things for you.'

Richard knew what that meant; they were the unofficial tax collectors.

Mr. Lukas began to walk away then turned, walked back to Richard, and stared deeply into Richard's eyes and soul. 'Be aware, Mr. Cole, *The Mistress of the Rock* is a possessive spirit; she does not give her affection easily.' Then almost as an afterthought, Lukas said his farewell. 'Enjoy your day, Mr. Cole.'

Richard said nothing, just watched as Mr. Lukas disappeared under the steps and into the approaching crowd. Then turning around, he hurried towards the waiting queues. There was a clear path into the water and he splashed through the waves to take up his place on the rope. The makeshift gate swung open and the first group came through and waited for his signal to go ahead. One by one they placed their money into the plastic storage box that stood by his side as he eased the first ten people down the rope. The sun became hotter, the water warmer, the queues longer, and Richard found himself employed.

CHAPTER TWELVE

AND STILL THEY COME

Richard was not certain how many people had made the journey down the ropes since he had opened that morning, he only knew that the ice box that contained the cash was almost full to the brim.

The hired help from Mr. Lukas kept making trips over to deposit more notes into the box, or was it just to check on the status of the cash? Richard couldn't be sure, he also couldn't be sure that the hired help wasn't helping themselves to any surplus as no one bothered giving out change. The crowd of people coming onto the beach just got bigger and bigger. It was also full of media groups but Richard detected an already diminishing enthusiasm for the story. As they say, *today's news is tomorrow's fish and chip wrappings.* In Cyprus, it would probably be kebabs.

Still, whatever the press was saying the people were listening to; more importantly, the place was getting all the attention that it had missed for some time. Maybe this is what *The Mistress of the Rock,* as Lukas called her wanted after all. More people to visit her birthplace, and Richard was delivering.

The hot sun burnt heavy on Richard's shoulders and body and he found himself refilling the sunscreen block constantly to avoid the inevitable sunburn. His face glistened with salty sea water, sun, and sweat. It was not the most attractive look, but people had not come to see him, they had come to see and touch the face of a Goddess. As Richard tightened the rope, he watched the people's various reactions. Most saw it as a publicity stunt or tourist exercise, but there were a few who appeared genuinely moved by the experience, as if inspired by this simple act; something reminiscent of a baptism.

Richard focused his attention on a girl, who was probably in her late teens, and definitely turned heads. She had light brown hair and was wearing a navy-blue bikini, which exposed a tan that showed her skin was used to the sun and a few tell-tale white bits. She moved slowly on the rope, almost delicately, as she edged her way along.

She approached the yellow ribbon that signified where the face of the goddess was and watched as the man in front—a Japanese tourist—pushed his head under the water and kissed the rock below. He emerged as quickly as he plunged, head dripping, nodding and smiling wildly. She took her turn and submerged almost in slow motion, dipping her head below the waves before rising again, her head soaking wet but the smile on her face electric. Whatever she had felt below the waters was clear on her face.

As the convoy of people continued after the Japanese man and the girl returned to the shore, Richard wondered for the umpteenth time if there really was something special about these rocks. He had not stopped for lunch, as the steady procession became endless, so he was grateful when the man from Costa's restaurant brought him a tray of sandwiches and a big bottle of cold water. Thanking him, Richard

128

reached down to take cash from the box, but the man waved his hand away, expecting no remuneration. After all, it was Richard, who was bringing him customers.

And still they came.

Peter, Sheila, and Julie arrived at the site after lunch; they called out to Richard, who was immersed in the sea and people. He couldn't hear them. As they got closer to the gate, Peter cried out to Richard again. This time he heard him and motioned to the men at the gate to let them through.

'Hi,' Richard was almost breathless.

'Christ, Richard, it's like a bloody frenzy. I didn't think there were this many people on the island. How are you going to cope?' Peter kept looking around at the crowds.

'Lukas sent over some of his guys, so they are helping me. And naturally, I think they are also keeping an eye on the money.' Richard tried to chat but he was too busy to stop.

'Where is it?' Peter queried.

'It's by my feet in this waterproof ice box.'

Julie kissed Richard and noticed instantly that his face was burning. Touching his skin gently with her hand, she took out a tissue and wiped some of the moisture away. He needed to replenish the sun block straight away.

'Can we have a go?' Sheila asked eagerly.

'Yes, but you must sneak in quick. There are a few in front of you who won't be pleased if they see you. Now, see where that yellow ribbon is? That's her head. Duck down in the water and kiss the stone below.' Richard eased the girls down the empty rope.

'Come on, Julie.' Sheila pressed herself and Julie forward as they waded into the water, leaving their sandals behind.

Richard held the rope to guide them.

Peter stood next to him, watching the activity. 'You do know the legend of this place, don't you?' He spoke quietly.

'What, the one about swimming naked around the rocks three times at midnight and you will find your true love?' Richard answered.

'Well, there is that one. There is also the one where if you're a woman, swim three times round the rock during full moon and you become twenty years younger.' Peter smiled as if the story was just too far-fetched.

For the first time that day, Richard relaxed, smiling at the idea of a woman swimming round the rocks to become younger. 'Don't tell Julie, or I will never get her out of the water.' Richard laughed aloud.

Peter joined in and with perfect timing delivered the punch line. 'And Sheila would have drowned by now.'

Now they were enjoying themselves.

They watched as first Sheila dipped her head into the water and then came out, soaked to the skin and dishevelled, followed by Julie, who also looked a little worse for wear after the ducking.

The women made their way back to shore, wondering what the men were so amused about, hopefully it was not their appearance.

It was arranged that Richard would meet Julie at Peter and Sheila's place after he finished at the rock. Tonight, they would sleepover at their friends'.

Richard's first real day had been a long one and exhausted, he shuffled to the front of the queue. 'Sorry, that's it for today. The sun is going in and the waves are getting bigger. The current is stronger too. Tomorrow…

Avriou... Tomorrow.   Goodbye, Yassas, Auf Wederzien, Sayonara, A Bien Tou... Au Revoir, and all things farewell.'

As he spoke, and before closing for the day, the hired help began to gather in their belongings.

The crowd dispersed slowly but there would be more days. Some still looked disappointed, but there was nothing Richard could do, as he was on the point of collapse. He also had cramps in one leg and sunburn all over him. He ached and he definitely needed a bath or a shower to get the day's toil off him. He dragged himself over to the water to get the rope. The metal poles were still fastened securely into the rocks, so they were staying put, but the rope needed to be brought in. It was just a simple knot and then a quick pull through, like unravelling a hose. Richard undid the knot and begun to walk to the next pole when he heard a woman's voice call his name.

'R   I   C   H   A   R   D...'

He looked around quickly but the area was empty. The sound was definitely a voice or it sounded like one but he was too tired to investigate further. He pulled the rope again and it went through the metal poles and cleared the loop. Richard took one last look around. The sea was cutting up rough now, so he returned to shore, just as the sun began to set.

Richard arrived at Peter and Sheila's twenty-five minutes after he left the rock and almost collapsed as the door opened.

Peter handed him a tumbler and the awaiting Scotch was sunk without ceremony, the ice tickling his tongue as he swallowed the lumps whole.

Julie had the bath ready and a hefty dollop of Radox Muscle Soak was foaming in the tub.

He stripped immediately, climbed in, and sank into the foaming water. So unlike the foaming waters he had been in all day. He shut his eyes and drifted almost into sleep but woke himself by rinsing his face with the face towel and running warm water down his back. Refreshed, he climbed out of the bath and looked at his sunburnt face and body. The handily placed after-sun was quickly employed and he soothed it onto his body. The heat could still be felt through his hands, so he smoothed the equally handy bottle of calamine all over his skin. That cooled him somewhat but he hated the pink streaks. Looking in the mirror, he smiled. He had worked hard today, but guess what? it started again tomorrow!

Julie was waiting for him when he emerged from the bathroom.

She was ready for the evening and looked very attractive. Her hair was neat and her dress sexy, in fact, one of his favourites. It was a flowing type silky cotton fabric patterned with butterflies and green streaks. The description did nothing for the dress, because it was only when she put it on that it transformed not only the garment but her as well.

Richard put on a short-sleeved white cotton shirt then slipped into his ironed cream-coloured cotton Chinos and completed the look with a pair of navy blue sneakers. He looked both smart and cool.

'Great, feeling better? You look better, another Scotch?' Peter said as soon as he saw Richard and offered him a new glass.

This time, he accepted it with thanks and sipped the liquor slowly.

'We're going to the Bunch of Grapes, which is just a five-minute walk from here, so we don't have to take the car. And that also means we can drink what we like, eh, Julie?' Sheila quipped and was already opening the door.

Peter and Richard walked behind the two women; both couples bonding in their own way.

'So, come on, tell me how much you made today?' Peter was eager to know.

'I honestly don't know, haven't counted it yet. But it must be close to a couple of thousand.'

'What, a couple of thousand! That much?'

'Sure, it must be. Well, work it out. Five to ten people every five minutes or so for four to five hours… it soon adds up.'

'Keep this up, Rich, and you will be... rich!'

Sheila and Julie moved up the slope to the restaurant. It was a lovely evening, the only noise the lament of the cicadas and the odd vehicle that drifted through the narrow roads, because apart from that there was nothing else. Entering the restaurant, every table was full; it was a good job that Peter had reserved theirs. Several of the patrons recognised Peter and waved to him and Sheila, whilst the curiosity for Peter's other two guests was clear, as most of the people recognised Richard. As they moved to take their seats, a round of spontaneous applause rang out around the room. Richard felt embarrassed and Julie didn't have a clue what to do next. She just stood and nodded and then Richard joined her. The applause subsided, the four returned to their table and the atmosphere in the restaurant returned to normal.

'Well, that's fantastic; all these people in here recognizing you. But you have done wonders for people's businesses and I hear the town is packed.' Sheila tried to contain her excitement.

'And it's not just here or Limassol, or at the Rocks, it's all over the island.' Peter confirmed the statement his wife had just made.

Julie endorsed it with a further comment that summed up the intensity. 'And all in a week...'

'I never imagined it would turn out like this.' Richard looked genuinely shocked.

Two waiters walked over to their table carrying a tray of crystal champagne glasses and a large chilled bottle of Bollinger. The gold foil top was unmistakable and the cork popped with some force as the expertly poured champagne entered the glasses.

Peter stood and toasted his friend. 'Here's to you, Richard, and your Goddess. Long may she reign.'

'To Aphrodite,' the chorus echoed around the vine-terraced restaurant and the party began in earnest.

Having sampled the chilled champagne and with the taste still fresh on his lips, Peter leaned across to Richard and spoke to him quietly. 'You'll probably get some sort of medal, from the President of tourism.' He smirked.

'Can we order now?' Sheila picked up the menu and handed it to Julie.

Peter did the same for Richard. 'Yes, come on, I'm starving... and they have great British food here so I am going to have my usual steak and kidney pie, with chips and some fresh vegetables, lovely.' Peter had made his choice.

'Are you not having a starter then, love?' Sheila queried as she had set her mind on the garlic mushrooms and pate for starter.

'Ok, yes, I will have a seafood cocktail. What about you, Richard?' Peter looked across at him.

'Nothing from the sea for me!'

Peter and Sheila laughed and Julie joined in.

Was it really that funny? Richard didn't care, he just knew that whatever he said now, people would listen. He was after all a celebrity, well, at least at this table he was.

The meal was delicious; the food a mixture of local produce, international, and British dishes, the cuisine easily rated one or two Michelin stars and was plentiful on the plates; in fact, Richard's steak was so large and succulent that it ran off the plate. The salad was crisp and the vegetables sweet and tasty. The 'piece de resistance' was the wine gravy that Richard poured liberally over his food; it was an exquisite taste that enriched the flavour of the meal. Julie's pasta bake Saint Jacque was also a triumph of the chef, served in a deep dish with wholesome pieces of seafood and fish that completed the ensemble. Peter's steak and kidney pie was cooked to perfection, light pastry on top of a deep dish of meat and kidney, presented on a separate plate from the other portions. Whilst Sheila had a lovely dish of Calves Liver and some sauté potatoes and greens. Over all, the menu was a huge success and so was the evening.

The hours ticked by rapidly and Richard was beginning to feel the day's efforts closing in on him, he had drunk copious amounts of beers and spirits and was now working his way through his second Sambuca, Peter was sipping his second or third Zivania, something he had grown accustomed to. They stood at the bar inside the restaurant, whilst the girls remained seated at the table.

Julie was also a little worse for wear with the drink. 'It will probably tail off by the time I get back.' She quipped.

'When are you leaving?' Sheila asked.

'I was able to change the flight. So I can leave Wednesday.'

'Why don't you stay? I mean, what's the point in going back early when you're here on holiday...' Sheila managed to somehow intimate that she enjoyed her company.

'If I go back now and get things sorted, as Richard says, he can get on with the business and not worry about me. When I return, he should have things in place and then we'll have a real holiday'

'I really hope so, but from what has happened so far, this thing is going to get bigger than you think.' Sheila held her friend's hand, real concern etched into her expression.

'That's what I'm afraid of too.' Julie understood the implications and how easy it could be for it to get out of hand. It was a very quick way to sober up.

'One for the road?' Peter stuttered his words a little.

'I think this road has come to a dead-end, love, so let's pay the bill and go home, we can have another coffee there.' Sheila had spoken.

Peter summoned the waiter with a wave of his hand. 'The bill, please.'

Richard reached into his pocket and took out a wad of notes. 'Our turn to pay.' He stretched his hand over to the waiter, who held a small china plate with the bill placed neatly folded in the middle.

The waiter spoke three words. 'Drinks are free.'

Richard nodded his thanks.

Peter stood and waved to the owner behind the bar then plonked himself down again in his seat.

Richard studied the bill, counted Ninety Euros, placed them onto the plate, and then added another ten.

The restaurant was almost empty as the party left for their short walk home. The stars and sky were bright and clear, but looking up to see them was not a good idea with the amount of drink that the four had supped, no, they would leave the night sky to the lovers.

Sheila poured the coffee, three were black, which was Julie's preferred mode of beverage, and the fourth a large glass of cold water.

Richard was the first to sober up, knowing he had to get up early in the morning. 'That was a great night, thanks.' Richard kissed Sheila on the cheek and shook hands with Peter.

'I will say goodnight then.' Julie repeated the process, only she kissed Peter on the cheek as well as Sheila and followed her husband. Peter called after Richard. 'I will come with you tomorrow, if you need help.'

'Thanks,' Richard's response was non-committal.

Julie opened the door to the guest's bedroom for Richard to crash out in.

The sunburn had returned and he needed to smooth after-sun into him badly. He washed in the sink and brushed his teeth as Julie undressed.

She put on a short nightdress then came across to him, removed the cap off the after-sun, and began to pour it into her hands, Slowly, the cold liquid eased into his burning skin; she rubbed gently, knowing how painful this sort of thing was.

Richard moaned from both the sensation of cooling down and her touch.

'You were a big celebrity tonight. All those people watching you. The women too, casting glances in your direction... made me quite jealous.'

'Why?' Richard turned around to look at his wife.

'Oh, I don't know, perhaps because you were getting all the attention.'

Moving his hands down, he stroked his wife's thigh then going all the way up, he pushed his fingers under the silky material of her nightdress and pulled it down, exposing her breasts.

'What are you doing?'

'I'm giving you a little attention.' He cupped his hand over her right breast and squeezed gently. 'After all, fame is a very powerful aphrodisiac.'

CHAPTER THIRTEEN

HIGH FINANCE

The sea was calm and smooth but a haze played over the water as Richard arrived at the rocks. A number of stall holders had begun to set up their stalls; tourist traders had certainly moved quickly. Within two days there was a new range of T-shirts with APHRODITE 'ROCKS' emblazoned across the front, and other merchandise branded in the same way adorned the front of the stalls. Anything to make a quick buck seemed to be the modus operandi. This was also true of the ice cream vans that had trebled their quota of vehicles over the past day or so.

The first coaches and buses were already parked, with both drivers occupied smoking a morning cigarette. Costa' restaurant was open and the tables were being placed outside for another busy day. Costa had to use more staff since Richard had started Goddess Dives, but he was more than adequately compensated by the extra trade being generated. In fact, the island began to rejuvenate as the phenomenon's appeal increased.

Richard collected the rope and with one of his hired help, a young man called Marcus, descended the rocks. Marcus was well built and in a black T-shirt combined with a muscular body, his fresh and youthful looks were a magnet for the young ladies, who flocked to the site.

A small crowd gathered at the foot of Aphrodite's Rock, watching the sun rise higher and burn off the sea mist and by the time Richard entered the water, the mist had all but disappeared. Together with Marcus, he waded out into the water and began to loop the rope through the metal poles, one by one knitting them through until they were tort and tight. Another batch of Lukas' men arrived to take up their positions and the day's work began.

As Richard came back to shore, he felt the cold-water splash against his legs; he was wearing a red T-shirt with sleeves to protect his skin and he also sported a bright sky blue baseball cap, which would help keep the sun away from his face a bit more. His shorts were the longest he could find but still the bottom part of his legs was bare so he applied large dollops of sun cream block to keep them protected as much as possible. The protection was necessary because the sun was already hotter than the previous day and it was only 8am.

The first lot to approach him was a couple in their fifties. He guided them slowly down the rope. The curiosity factor of the Goddess under the Sea was something that appealed to all ages and it was clear that Richard had uncovered a monster. Could he control it? He pondered this thought as more and more people plied their way down the rope.

After an hour, Peter arrived carrying a large picnic basket. Without asking, he poured his pal a large plastic beaker of tea.

'Oh tea,' Richard said, pleased to see him and taking the beaker, drank gratefully and quickly. 'You can't beat tea on a day like today.'

'Shall I take over for a while? Give you a break?' Peter offered.

'Thanks, could do with five minutes. The money is in the ice box; when the boys come across lift the lid so they can see inside then drop the notes in, ok? That seems to satisfy them, though, God knows why.' Richard offered his hand to Peter and tapped his back in gratitude.

He walked away from the gate and out on the beach, found a patch of shade near the steps, and sat down. It was a slightly raised area, so he had a good vantage point to see most things, the ropes were busy with people going up and down them, and the makeshift gate had a queue behind it that stretched past the steps. Lukas' men were all engaged in keeping the operation moving, whilst Peter was really enjoying himself chatting to the people and networking, if that's what one would call it. Richard looked out across the beach. The sea was a deep blue and almost transparent when the sun bounced off the surface. There were a few people bobbing up and down in the waves close to the shore, not really swimming, just using the water to cool down in.

One of the difficulties about swimming near the rocks was the current, which was not steady, having wild moods and could become volatile at any moment. Swimming was perhaps not the best thing to do; it also stopped the legend hunters from trying to get their wishes. But Goddess Dives didn't prove problematical, so it was probably why Lukas had encouraged the idea.

As Richard sat on the stones, he saw a figure in the water. It was further out at sea, the glare of the sun making it difficult to see clearly. Richard tried to shade his eyes but sweat ran down his hair and into his eyes, the sun block melting on his face. The figure came closer to the shore even if still a way off. Richard stood up, trying to catch a better sight of it. It looked like someone was lying on a surf board, paddling towards shore. He couldn't make it out, so he looked around for someone who might have binoculars, but there was no one. He moved down the slope but the masses stopped him from seeing more and obstructed his view. He went back to the slope but the figure was gone. He looked again. There was no one there. He returned to the queues.

Peter was busy but appeared to not need his help as his advantage of speaking Greek was also paying off. He was in fact becoming a big asset.

'Can you stay longer, Pete?' Richard asked.

'Sure, I'm enjoying this. What with all these half-naked women getting close to me, it's a real pleasure.' he was grinning wildly.

The rest of the morning passed quickly and so did the afternoon, Richard's shirt had protected him from some of the sunburn but the back of his legs had turned scarlet and looked very sore. He had set a time of five for the last dives of the day, and it was close to that as the next crowd lined up. These people were a group in their thirties and they looked Danish, he recognised some words from his days in the army when he worked with some Danes.

Peter held the rope and Richard watched the last girl turn away, having ducked down into the water. Then she ducked down again and then again, in a sort of panic.

Richard went out to her. 'What's the matter?' He asked, as she girl emerged from the water.

'My bracelet, it is on the rocks and I can't reach it.' She spoke good English.

'Okay, I will get it.' Richard quickly returned to shore and grabbed his diver's mask and donned it, as the girl stood beside him. He pushed his head under the water. It was cold but he had a clear sight and immediately noticed the bracelet balancing on the rock. Richard reached down, almost touching it. He stretched his hand further and as he did the rock's smooth yellow surface melted away and the face of a woman appeared in its place. He could see her clearly. He grabbed the bracelet and emerged, gave the bracelet to the girl and then dived down again. The face was gone.

Could it have been the girl's reflection from above as he dived down into the water? No, this was definitely a different face. Startled by the apparition he waded back towards Peter, unsure of what had happened. The sun must be affecting him more than he cared to admit.

It was Tuesday night; Julie and Sheila had decided to stay at the apartment. Sheila had brought more of Julie's favourite cakes and biscuits and in between packing they munched away at them. Peter and Richard had decided on a quick beer at the pub up the road from the apartment.

It was a clear evening and the tourists were out in force, much of the restaurant trade happened at around this time and as Peter and Richard walked the few hundred yards to the pub, the front men from the restaurants propositioned them with free wine with their meal if they ate at their particular establishment, or a free desert. Peter nodded his thanks and walked on as the front men waited for their next victims to enter their domain. They sat in a quiet corner of the bar. There were a couple of locals and an ex pat, who was far too engaged reading a newspaper to notice them. The headline read 'Another fifty-five dead in Baghdad Bombing'. Richard and Peter supped quietly.

'Busy day, eh?' In his own way, Richard was asking Peter if he had enjoyed it.

'Think so?' It was an odd reply to a question that only need a yes, but Peter justified it with his next statement. 'We're not even in high season yet. How do you think you will cope when it really does get busy?'

'I suppose I'll hire more hands, or maybe Lukas will send some.' Richard was not the best at business finance; he was okay when it came to saving money, but not when it came to managing it.

'You need to put a business plan together, because the amount of money this place might eventually take could be phenomenal. And it doesn't take anything to upkeep, so it's just a case of collecting the cash every day. It's a business miracle.' Peter was buzzing now.

'You reckon?' Richard was coming to the realisation that what he had created was indeed a monster.

'Yes… Richard, you are printing money there. How much did you take today?' Peter didn't need convincing; he just wanted to hear it.

'Two thousand, I counted it when I got home.'

'Incredible; that's twice as much as most Cypriots make in a month and you took that in a day.'

'I do have to give half to Lukas, remember? So it would have been two grand.'

'Unbelievable; you made a thousand in a day.' Peter was starting to add up the figures.

'I know because I still can't believe it. I don't have any overheads either; it's just pure profit.'

'Then apart from that you're on your way to your first million, what else is new?' Peter decided to change the finance subject.

Richard relaxed a little. 'I have to find an apartment by the end of the week; our stay is over so if you know of a place, will you let me know?'

'With that kind of cash, you could stay at the Aphrodite Hills. It's beautiful and just five minutes from the rocks. But I think you would be better off staying with us. I can keep an eye on you then.' Peter smiled.

'That's a nice thought, and thanks, but I think I'll look for somewhere close to the rocks, as you say. Another beer? My shout.'

Peter handed him his glass. 'I should bloody well think so.' He laughed loudly as Richard collected the glass and walked to the bar.

Richard did not mention the face on the rocks; putting it down to too much sun. Tomorrow he would need a bigger hat.

Julie's flight was in the early hours of the morning; four am was her check in at Paphos, so neither wanting to be late, they said their goodbyes to Peter and Sheila.

Peter insisted again that Richard should consider staying with them but Richard continued resisting, also knowing full well that once Julie had him alone in the car she too would insist on him staying with them.

They made love quickly, the sort that fell under the heading of quickie because both needed to rest. And although they would soon be apart, there was no long drawn out foreplay, just instant passion and then straight to sleep. It was concise and a little crude but it was the best either could offer in the moment.

The alarm bells rang simultaneously, and Julie stepped out of her night-clothes and into her travelling gear.

Richard climbed into his jeans and a shirt automatically.

It was dark outside when they loaded the hired car and quietly set out, getting through the tourist area in ten minutes. The last few clubs were shutting down their lights, though one or two seemed to be still in full swing. They passed the remnants of a few drunken souls as they flashed by the car windows making their way back to their respective hotels and apartments.

Out on the Paphos highway the car picked up speed, the fuel indicator showing half full. Richard would need to top up later. He had also packed his gear for the day. He would just stop for breakfast and then go to work. Work on holiday, such a strange expression.

As they passed the rocks, Julie gave Richard a knowing smile, as if to say, 'I know this is where you work.'

They had only passed one truck with animals in the back on the way; either pigs or goats on route to somewhere, and a couple of late night taxis. But near the airport traffic was considerably busier; cars, coaches, vans, all heading in the same direction and the arc and floodlights shone brightly across the landscape.

The runway could be seen clearly in the distance, and a couple of planes were on it awaiting take-off. Richard parked the car in the short stay parking area and moved swiftly for a trolley, placing Julie's hand luggage and case on it and together they walked towards the doors.

The activity inside was not prolific but there were already a number of people lined up in front of the boards and behind the yellow line. The check-in desks, branded with mostly charter-based carriers were lit and a couple of young uniformed Cypriot girls sat behind two of them.

Julie waited with Richard for their turn to move up to the yellow line. The couple in front of them looked as if they were well over the luggage limit, but their bags were heaved onto the scales with no problem then eased down the conveyor belt to the luggage handlers and then onto the plane. It was automation at its finest, except when it came to the manual handling of the cases.

Richard took Julie's case and hauled it onto the scales.

The girl behind the counter recognized him and smiled. Julie was not happy at the thought of her husband alone on an island where the women outnumbered men four to one; and with the newfound celebrity status it was a potent combination. But she had made up her mind to go and she needed to trust him, so she handed her passport over and with it her answers to the obligatory security questions.

'Shall we go for coffee?' Richard asked.

'No, I'm fine, but you have one I'll go through now and have a look around in duty-free.'

'You have almost two hours.' Richard wanted to know why.

'No, it's ok, let me go now.' Julie was fighting hard to stop the tears. The last few days came rushing back, even as she tried to keep it in. And she couldn't tell him she didn't want to go, that she would rather stay.

'What is it, love?' Richard's concern was heartfelt.

'It's nothing… I will be fine; you know how nervous I get flying.'

He held her tight in his arms and then felt her pull away.

She kissed him again and again, and then she was gone, off through immigration and out of sight.

Richard left the airport, not happy. He had indeed sacrificed his holiday for a dream and now he had sacrificed his wife too, or so it seemed. For the first time in days he felt melancholic; he had not wanted Julie to go, but now she had, and there was nothing else to do but get on with the job.

But once he was inside his car, the melancholy disappeared; he was on his own and that meant freedom, well, a sort of freedom. The first thing he needed to do was get his head clear and that meant a fresh coffee. Yes, that was the first thing.

The text clicked on the cell and he opened it.

MISSING YOU ALREADY, JULES XXX

Richard responded in his best melodramatic Ghost movie style, DITTO.

CHAPTER FOURTEEN

DID YOU SEE HER?

Richard left the airport road, a journey he had not expected to make when he arrived just over a week ago. One usually arrives and leaves only once from the airport on holiday, but Richard's, like Julie's, was over. He drove back along the road and on the motorway while it was still dark, but cracks of light were beginning to filter through the night clouds, the moon's reflection bathing them with a sort of incandescent light within. The odd car passed him and another lorry filled with animals on route to the here-after.

He turned off the highway and down the side road. Costa' restaurant was still in darkness and the roadside was empty. The morning sea air was chilly as he parked the car off the road. He stood at the edge and surveyed his landscape, because in a funny kind of way he felt it was his, or at the very least the tenant.

The sun was not in the sky, just the moon. It slipped through the clouds one by one as if it was playing a form of celestial hide-and-seek, first hiding then chasing them. The sea breeze whisked through the rolling water and the echoing waves duly obliged by crashing into the rocks. The shoreline was opaque in the darkness and it was really only the sound of the crashing waves that acknowledged the sea below. As he stood looking out to the sea he could not yet see, he thought about the figure on the surfboard and the face in the rock.

Strange that he had witnessed two separate incidents that he could not explain properly. Maybe this place really was mystical; maybe there was true magic in the rocks. He had definitely seen something on the face of that girl who emerged from the water, her face had been alive with the experience, or was it simply an overactive imagination, in overdrive from the hype of it all? He sat on the edge just watching the sea below him, he didn't feel cold.

A plane soared into the sky, high above him. He checked his watch, was it Julie's? It could be.

Right on queue, the sun rose in the horizon, splitting the night to herald the beginning of another hot day. The lights flickered on across the road from where he sat, Costa' restaurant was open. It was time for that coffee.

Richard sat with Costa and drank a large mug of Nescafe, while also tucking into a Haloumi and Lountza toasted sandwich that Costa had made for him.

The first buses arrived around 7am. The rocks were now a last stop for some tourists who wanted a couple of quick early morning shots before making their way to the airport. The restaurant was again doing good trade. One of the traders from the stalls recognised him and walked over. He didn't speak English well, but he didn't need to as he handed Richard a complimentary bright purple *Aphrodite Rocks* T-shirt. Richard thanked him and tucked it into his bag then he waited for the group in the restaurant to clear and sat back in his seat and glanced around.

The faded mural on the walls had not been touched, most of the posters were also untouched, but there was something different about the place. He watched as the waiters moved around like dancers, as if a new lease of life had been birthed within the place. The first night that Julie and he had been here, the restaurant atmosphere had been nothing special, the hospitality was fine but not over the top, the food good, but enthusiasm had been lacking. There was nothing special. But it had all changed with Richard's discovery, and that was it! Although the place below was special, no one had appreciated it, just another name on a map. He, Richard, had made it unique again. A new breath of life was breathed into it and the staleness had vanished.

Within an hour, the crowds began to arrive. There was now a noticeable tourist stream, which had become the main audience. The local market was not yet in evidence, areas such as Ayia Napa, Larnaca, Troodos, Platres, and many of the nearby villages as well as the Capital, Nicosia, had not visited thus far. Still, it was only a week after all and as Julie had so eloquently and succinctly put it confirming Peter's earlier repeated statement 'We are not in high season yet!'

Everything was in place. He had become adept at making sure the site ran properly, having his staff, or rather, Lukas' staff in place and the makeshift gate was already swinging back and forth with every new visitor.

Peter arrived at just after 9:00am; again coming prepared with a big box of food and drink. He had also sneaked a couple of large beers in, but Richard wasn't ready for those. He needed to keep his head in full working order, did not want any distractions, or surprises. No, he had to concentrate on the job in hand.

Peter was a good aid, having a friendly banter with the customers and knew how to keep the line moving well, in fact, it was moving so well that they were able to process many more people as the hours ticked by. The money mounted up in the box, Peter encouraged Richard to keep covering himself with sun block, as Richard tended to forget. Peter was doing Julie's job now.

The sun was like a hot button in the sky; and with no clouds for shade it burnt hot and heavy down onto the shore. The rocks were the only shade to speak of and many of the tourists had set up their towels and sunshades as close to them as possible to protect themselves from the burning sun as they queued to see the Goddess.

'Time for a break?' Richard encouraged.

'Ok,' Peter nodded his approval at the suggestion. And he looked like he needed it too, as the day's efforts were also beginning to have their effects on him. It was in no way easier working in the intense heat even if you were more acclimatised than others.

Midday is the time when a lot of Cypriots pack up and go home for their afternoon siesta; a quaint custom that allows them to sleep through the hottest hours of the day before returning to work later in the afternoon. The tourist areas don't operate like this but some Cypriot businesses do. Richard motioned to Marcus to put two men in place and they duly obliged. He didn't worry about them stealing any cash anymore; he had come to trust them.

They sat in the shade of the steps, just as he had done the previous day. The cold beer was welcomed now and the fresh sandwiches made for a perfect packed lunch. He glanced at his watch; he would wait another couple of hours and then ring Julie, let her rest a while longer.

'Have you had any luck finding a place yet?' Pete asked.

'To be honest, I haven't looked. But I will probably go for somewhere local so I don't have far to travel. You said the Aphrodite Hills was a fantastic place, maybe I'll go there.' Richard took another bite from his sandwich.

'Yes, it's fabulous and it has a wonderful golf course. Do you play?'

'No, never tried, and I don't think I'd be very good all that eye hand co-ordination. Not my sort of thing.'

'I can teach you if you like, as you're going to be here a while.'

'Thanks, but the way this is going I'm not going to have time, am I? Considering you say we are not in high season yet.'

'Yes, I think this is going to take over your life; what happens then?'

'I don't know.' Richard took a long swig from the beer, the cold liquid refreshing his dry mouth then wiped the remains of the sandwich with his hand.

Incredibly, the temperature had risen another three or four degrees since they had first sat down.

Peter was the first to get up and walk back to the awaiting crowds. If anything, the numbers had swollen up during the short respite that they had taken. Richard put the rubbish he had collected into a bag, began to walk back, and then stopped.

In the water ahead of him, he saw a woman. She was swimming slowly towards the shore, her hair shimmering in the sunlight and her tanned dark golden brown shoulders visible above the waves. He couldn't see her face clearly, but the way she swam was so elegant, with so much finesse it was like she was stroking the water, the waves moving slowly across her with every movement of her hand. She came closer to the beach and then walked out. Her body was almost straight, yet she had a figure that most women would die for, a hint of curves and subtlety in her shape. She flicked the shaggy mane of her dark brown hair across her face and for the first time, Richard saw her eyes; they were blue. Like the sea, they were deep and shone back as if reflecting within themselves. He guessed she might be in her twenties, yet there was a youthfulness about her that perhaps made her seem even younger, portraying a vision in virtue and a lesson in lust. She was beautiful and sensuous, her movement so majestic and stylish, she sashayed and wiggled her hips in harmony as the two-piece light brown suit she wore accentuated all of her body, delivering an image of desire so powerful that Richard found himself moving towards her. But just as quickly as she emerged on the sea-shore, she was gone, lost in the crowd. Richard tried to find her and pushed through to the sand but there was no sign of her. He looked again.

It was then that Peter called out to him 'Hey, we need you over here.'

Richard acknowledged Peter and walked as fast as he could in the heat back towards him, while glancing around to see if he could still see the one who had so captivated him. 'Sorry, I saw a girl in the water.'

'Drowning, was she?' Peter's hint at sarcasm was lost.

Richard returned to the group in front of him and began to collect the cash again.

It was four pm when Richard called Julie.

She had slept for a couple of hours and been awake for a while waiting to hear from him.

'Hi, how are you, how was the flight, are you okay, how's Molly?'

He asked questions so quickly that she couldn't respond fast enough, so she just said. 'Good, fine, good, she's out.'

Richard realised that his annoying habit of not letting anyone else speak was also true of his phone conversations; he shut up and waited for Julie to say her piece.

'Everything is fine, but you have so much mail here. God knows how people got hold of our address and number, but they have. You have letters from TV companies and Media agents, who want you to advertise, travel companies who want you to sponsor them, or they to sponsor you. There's even a letter from a film company, who want to do a movie about you and the rocks.'

Richard could only respond with 'Oh my God.'

'Molly left me a pile of numbers from people who want you to call them. I haven't even looked at those yet. I will get around to them tomorrow and let you know what they say, ok? Apart from that I miss you and love you lots.'

'I do too, love, and don't know what to say. Where is Molly?'

'She went to stay with her friend Lucy; she said she wanted some peace.'

'Tell her sorry for me, will you?' Richard wanted his daughter on his side too.

'It's fine, she's fine, I think she liked all the attention at first but then it got too much; Matthew came back for a while but now he's gone too, off with his friends to Cornwall.

What about you, have you found anywhere to stay yet? I think Peter's offer is a good idea, that way you'd have company too.'

'I think you're right, as I'm also considering making him a partner in Goddess Dives, giving him some of the profits too of course. He has helped me so much and he's really good with the customers.'

'That is a great idea. He would be a great asset and he knows the language and the country.'

'Exactly, and he's been a good pal too. So has Sheila.'

'You're breaking up a bit,' the phone line was intermittent with its signal. 'I better go now, make a start on some of these letters. Call me tomorrow, okay? Love you.'

'Me too, Jules, speak tomorrow.' The cell clicked dead. It was an awful sound, a faint click that announced that they were no longer in touch, because once their conversation was over the miles that separated them returned. The phone could be a cruel tool of communication.

Richard looked down the beach; the crowd was still large, but he would be there for only another hour. Then he would drive back to the apartment and maybe start looking for a new place, but if Peter offered again, he would take it. Julie's conversation had surprised and shocked him, all those letters and messages from people who wanted to do business, or work, or just talk to him. It made him grin with pride. Fame certainly was powerful, no matter who you were.

Just as daybreak is different every day at Aphrodite's Rock; so too is sunset, in fact, sunsets are perhaps even more spectacular than dawn, because they bring together colours that can only be seen then. Like a painter mixing his paints on his palette, the sun and Mother Nature combine to mix an array of colours that can't be captured by any canvas or photograph, the image never true enough to the live display. The rocks too play their part, providing a scenic backdrop in a pattern of oranges and yellows that enhance the perpetual blues of the Mediterranean, so that if they were ever mixed together they would make the most vibrant and verdant green. Like the pastures of heaven.

Richard appreciated this special time. 'This is the best time of the day, sunset. It's awesome, so beautiful, and so mystical.'

'Yes'. Peter was not so enthused. 'No more mystery women then?'

'No.' The curt answer told Peter to drop the subject. 'Ready; let's go. I'm tired, shattered, and bloody sunburnt again.'

'Rich, honestly, you are going to need to sort this out better, mate. It's too much for you to do on your own.' Peter's look of concern was genuine, noticing his friend's suffering from the heat and the worry of trying to make it all work out. What seemed like a simple exercise was turning into a logistical nightmare.

'Yes, you're right, and Julie has just told me there's a pile of letters and phone calls waiting from people who want to work with me; but not tonight, I am totally shattered and I need to cool down.' Richard moved to collect the ice box from the water and turned to hand it to Peter. Off in the distance he saw what looked like the girl from earlier in the day, walking up the beach, away from him. 'Hang on, be right back.' He began to move quickly towards the girl.

'Now, where are you going?' Peter followed him, before he got lost in the departing crowd, then he returned to the rocks.

Richard cleared his path through to the shore but the girl was too far away and was soon out of sight. He got back as Peter was folding the rope. 'Did you see her?' He asked anxiously.

'See who?'

'Sorry, I thought I saw someone.' Richard took the rope in his hands.

'What, another mystery woman?'

'No, the same one.'

Richard's answer threw Peter off a bit and not really knowing what to say next, he chose to say nothing.

With the site closed, they walked together up the shore, towards the steps, and just as they left the beach and climbed the steps, behind them, further up the beach, the girl turned around and walked back towards the rocks.

CHAPTER FIFTEEN

PARTNERS

Richard arrived back at the apartment around 7:00pm, he stopped to get some last-minute supplies, which he would cook tonight and then call a few places but if he couldn't find anywhere he liked, he would call Peter after his shower and take him up on his offer. He had burnt again but it didn't seem as bad. Perhaps his skin was getting used to it, but still, he needed to cover up more. He could not afford to become ill.

The shower was hot; the solar-heated water was an energy-efficient way of heating. If only they would do this in England, but not likely, not with the British weather. He thought for a moment about Julie, and home, and how much he was missing her. They had never been separated like this, except when he was in the army and then it was a different kind of worry; that had been a survival worry, this worry was uncertainty, and all that held for them both.

He let the water run over him, then he massaged the soapy foaming lather into his burnt shoulders, legs, and thighs, and turned the heat up. He had read somewhere that really hot water took some of the sting out of sunburn. It sounded logical but in practice was stupid, as he almost burnt his foot as extra heat poured out of the tap. It was time to leave the

159

shower, which now resembled a steam bath, with water vapour rising like a misty fog, until he opened the window and it escaped through the hole.

Richard put on his bathrobe and made his way to the bedroom. He picked up Aphrodite's figurine and looked at it, then put it back. As he dried himself, he opened the pages of the book that Julie had left, and began to skip though the pages. Most of the images were ones he saw daily, but there were some that were new to him. Still wet, he lay on the bed and read the book, his body ached as his muscles relaxed. Then he grabbed the phone because if he lay there any longer he would fall asleep.

'Hi, Pete. No, no, I'm fine. Had my shower and just about to cook something. Pete, I wanted to ask you something.'

'Err, it's not about the girl you saw on the beach, is it? Cos' I didn't see her, even though there were hundreds that I did see.'

'No, it's not that, but she was stunning. So beautiful, and I only saw her for a few seconds too...'

'Hey, steady on mate... your wife's only been gone two days and you're already fantasizing...' Peter laughed nervously. 'I think you caught a little too much sun, Rich.'

'Don't tell Sheila about her, or she will be on the phone to Julie right away, and I don't want that worry.' Richard emphasised the statement.

'No, no problem, your secret is safe with me. So, what can I do for you?'

'There was something I wanted to ask, well, two things actually. Is the offer of staying with you still open; just until I get settled out here and Julie is back? And secondly, how would you like to become my partner in Goddess Dives?'

'What... Me?'

'Yes, you. You are really good at the site. And you know the language, you have a real gift when it comes to chatting to the people, and I get on well with you.'

'The offer to stay is open and it would have been even if you hadn't offered me a partnership. And second, I think the idea of being with you on this venture is just fantastic. I think the people at the aerodrome were looking to get rid of me anyway; the joyride thing has given them a reason now... So this is just great... Yes of course I accept, Rich. Should I come get you now?'

'No, thanks, I've paid till Saturday, so I'll stay until then. Things to sort out here, but Saturday night will be good, if that's ok with you.'

'Fine, then on Sunday I will cook Souvla. That's a barbecue to you.'

'Fantastic, sounds great. And thanks. See you there tomorrow about 9, ok?'

'No. I will be there at 8am, I'm working now.' Peter laughed loudly then putting the cell down, he looked at Sheila, who was watching TV. 'He wants me to be a partner.'

Sheila stopped and looked across towards him. Her calculator had already clicked into gear in her brain and began totalling up the money that was on offer at the site and how much Peter could get from it. That would certainly make a difference to their circumstances; pity there wasn't a way for it to be just Peter's. 'Make sure you get a good percentage.' She said and turned back to the TV, a sly smile sweeping over her lips.

'Well, that's that; sorted.' Richard returned to his book and lay back on the bed.

The beach was quiet, too quiet for this time of day. Richard glanced at his watch, it was just after eleven but there were only a few people around. He walked along the shoreline as the waves splashed around his feet then walked into the waves and let the cold sea water wash over them. He waded in a little deeper, letting the water move up his body. As he turned to walk back to shore he heard the voice again, the same voice he had heard at the rocks.

'R i c h a r d... R i c h a r d...'

He looked around, but there was no one around. He moved out of the water and lay back on the sand, shut his eyes, and then snapped them open again as he sensed someone there.

Standing over him was the girl from the beach.

He looked up at her as the sun reflected against his eyes and dazzled him. 'It's you. What's your name? Pos se lene?'

She smiled and moved away.

Richard began to run after her.

She turned to the water and dived into the waves.

Richard swam after her, trying to reach her, but she kept moving away, as if teasing him. Unable to keep up, he struggled against the waves as she moved further away. His arms felt heavy against the awesome power and his body ached. Something below the water grabbed him and gave him a quick Jaws-like jerk. There was a pause, almost a hesitant moment, as he bobbed up and down then came a greater pull. As the water sucked him in, he was grabbed and dragged downwards. Fighting to breathe, he wrestled against the current to find air but instead found only liquid. Submerged below the water, his body spiralled and twisted as something pulled down into the depths. He opened his eyes, realising that the rocks were dragging him down, sucking him in, deeper and deeper into them. He gasped for air. His breath nearly gone, he shut his eyes and then opened them again.

The face he had seen before appeared on the rocks. It was 'Her', the face of the girl from the beach; he tried to call out but lost consciousness as he began to drown, his body limp, being sucked down into the rocks. 'NO, NO, NO...' He screamed.

It was a dream so vivid, so real, and terrifying that he was sure the neighbours had heard him. And the sweat dripping from him only confirmed what an ordeal he had just experienced. He sat up and looked at the clock, 3:30am. He had to be up in two and a half hours and he had only just gone to sleep, or so it seemed.

The fetid sleep made him rise early. He showered again, dressed, and made toast and coffee. He got himself ready and then sat out on the balcony, watching the tide ebb and flow against the shore. The beach sweeper was also up early, he was cleaning the sand and the area around the deck chairs and beach umbrellas, brushing the clean sand and smoothing it again before returning the broom to the start.

Wearily, Richard watched the early morning joggers kicking up little bits of sand as they moved along the beach, their fitness routine part of their daily ritual. Out at sea, he scanned the convoy of containers lying off anchor, awaiting their chance to enter port. Ships of all sizes dotted the sea lanes; evidence that Limassol's port was a busy place. Richard was about to close the balcony door when he registered a woman running along the shore. He couldn't see her well enough and was just about to leave the balcony when she looked straight at him. It was the girl from the shore and the girl in his dream. He stood still, watching as she moved silently up the beach, away from him. He wanted to follow her, but knew that by the time he got down there she would be gone. But next time he saw her he would be ready. Richard loaded the camera with new batteries and checked that it worked as he clicked a couple of images of the seafront. Then he loaded up his gear and got ready for work.

Peter was at the rocks early. It was after all a short distance from Pissouri, so it was logical that he would be there first. But that wasn't the only reason, he was also eager to get started in his new job. He had found something that would keep him occupied and entertained, and was getting paid for it too Although no actual money had been discussed as yet, he could see that the way things were going he would be better off than most people he knew. For this venture, and the possibilities it offered were astounding.

The morning was off to a good start; two coaches full of Japanese tourists parked at the top of the road were just waiting to disembark their passengers. But Peter wasn't prepared to let them down yet, he needed to have Richard and the others with him. As he waited for them to arrive, he studied the set up and how the poles were anchored. They were designed to get people safely around them, but it was not the most efficient way. Surely, there was another method that would not only get people around safely but also increase the numbers. And in this heat, they needed a way to process crowds quicker to make it easier for everyone. He looked at the poles again and realised that they formed a sort of corral, a semi-square that moved people around its perimeter and along the ropes. If they could create a way to move people in opposite directions so that as one went down another came up it would solve a few dilemmas.

Richard parked the car, got out, and walked across to Costa.

Peter sat on one of the benches, his dark sunglasses shimmering against the morning sun. 'Good morning.' He was first to speak.

'Hi, ready then?' Richard was not great in the mornings. Julie used to say that he was allergic to them, especially when it meant he had to converse with people.

'Yes, all set. Rich, I've been thinking while sitting here about how we can get more people to the dive.' Peter announced eagerly.

'Oh, yeah, I've been worrying about that too. We don't have enough hours in the day and they just keep on coming, which is great for us, so any ideas are most welcome.'

'Ok, well, let me have a think again and then we can try something.'

'I knew that making you a partner was a good idea. Oh, and we have to sort out the cash percentage part as well, I was thinking maybe sixty forty.'

'Yes, sixty for me seems fair.' Peter grinned.

'Cheeky bastard, I'm the sixty.' Richard made sure he knew what he meant, even in jest, and then the two walked down to the rocks.

They had a crowd waiting for them, so the day's events were now of paramount importance, and Richard's bad nightmare was forgotten and it looked like another scorcher.

As the coaches emptied their passengers, the two of them were open for business just as the first tourists emerged on the shore. Lukas's men had not arrived yet, but they couldn't keep their audience waiting any longer.

Peter's idea had better come soon, Richard thought, *we need to sort this out and quick.*

By 8am the others arrived and brought with them two new helpers, Achilles and Paris, celebrated names of two Greek mythology heroes. It was a custom for both Greek and Cypriot kids to be named after ancient heroes like Alexander or Hercules, or just called after their Father's Father, like 'Nicos or Nick, or Niki. or Nicola, or anything else that began with Nic. Or they would be called after a city, like Athena for Athens; it was all deep-rooted in Greek and Cypriot culture and there were probably ten thousand Aphrodites on the island, but Richard's interest was with only the one; the one who at the moment was paying his salary.

The morning went quickly and as they stopped for lunch, Peter began to draw on a white napkin the design that had been floating in his head.

Richard watched him draw one design then cross it out, then another, then cross that one out too. He also kept his camera close by, just in case he saw something, or someone.

Peter drew the design again; then separated it with a solid black line right down the middle. By partitioning the corral, he could divide the people into two groups. That way, he could send one lot up in one direction and the other in the opposite direction. It was simple but brilliant. The only difficulty was the dive itself; he needed someone at the ribbon to make sure that only one person at a time dived. That would need supervision.

'So what have you come up with then?'

'This! I think if we separate the ropes in this way, we can divide the people in half with one lot going one way and the other the opposite way. The only setback is that we need someone at the yellow ribbon, to make sure that only one person dives.'

'That could work, and we would double the amount of people on the ropes too. What do you need?'

'Do you still have the poles and rope I gave you?'

'Yes. Costa has them here. He's been looking after them for me.'

'Great. When we close tonight, we'll try to set it up. I'm just a bit worried about the supervision, it means spending a long time in the water for someone.'

'We can rotate, and with Lukas' guys, you, and me we will be able to cover it.'

'Do you think they will go for it?' Peter wasn't convinced that Lukas' men would.

'I'm sure they will, but I will have a word and see what they say first. Besides, they might like the idea of cooling down in the water.' Richard shook Peter's hand. 'Yep, I knew that making you a partner was a good idea, especially when I only have to give you thirty percent.'

'What?' Peter looked shocked.

'Only joking, but you should see your face. Now finish your sandwich, we have customers to see.'

By 5:00pm most people at the rocks were either hot or tired, or both. They had had a busy day and the crowd had gone away satisfied. There was also the odd journalist or two who was still looking for a story but the mainstream news stations had now had enough of the rocks. But it wasn't about the media for Richard; it was about a promise to a lady, whom he felt deeply obligated to, even if that lady was just a myth.

Richard carried the poles into the water and set them up as Peter had directed. Peter held the other one and planted it into the seabed. Richard reciprocated. The divide was right down the middle and the rope extended across through the poles and back to the shore. There was a bit of spare rope so Peter tied that around a rock near the shore, it tightened it, and they were able to gauge how the new setup would work. There was a clear divide that allowed people to move in opposite directions.

Peter called Marcus and his friends over and one set went one way whilst the other went in the opposite direction, just as he had drawn on the napkin. Richard stood at the centre, in the middle where the ribbon was. He held the rope and waited as first Marcus and then Achilles approached, it was working. As one group made their way up so the other made their way down; both groups pausing as they waited their turn to duck into the water before emerging and moving on. It was as Peter put it with a satisfied grin, poetry in motion.

CHAPTER SIXTEEN

SOUVLA AND SHARES

Saturday came quick and fast; the new system was working well and they were able to get through far larger numbers; what they still needed to do was to secure the poles in the rocks in the same way that the other four were, but this would have to suffice for the time being. Richard would speak to Mr. Lukas about it. Strange, he had not seen anything of Lukas since the last time he had been at the rocks and given him his warning about 'The Mistress of the Rock'. He hadn't even been around to see how they were getting on; all he knew was the guys took their share each day, which was duly counted out and Richard checked.

There was no official way to see exactly how many people went up and down the ropes; and there was no way to give out tickets for this. It was done on trust. In effect, a lot of the island's business was conducted the same way, purely on trust. There was no crime to speak of, just the tourists got turned over, and some foreign nationals; but in general Greeks didn't rob or murder Greeks unless it was something personal. The only real challenge they faced in that department was the alarming road deaths, which are some of the highest in Europe per head. Speed and the refusal to wear seatbelts were the main cause of the fatalities and for motorcyclists, the most vulnerable group of all, a lack of helmets, or rather, also not wearing them; that and a bit of road ignorance, which Richard had met more than a few times since his arrival.

Richard packed his suitcase and placed his laptop in its bag. How different things would have been if he hadn't downloaded those pictures. How fate plays with you, especially when you least expect it. Still, that was that and because of it his life had changed. While he waited for Peter to arrive, he saw he had time to ring Julie. But as he picked up the telephone and lifted it to his ear, and before he dialled the number the same female voice he heard on the beach was calling him.

'RICHARD, RICHARD...'

He threw the phone to the floor; this was not funny anymore.

Peter knocked.

Richard opened the door ushered his mate in and said nothing about the voice. They collected the suitcase and extra bags and left the apartment. Passing reception, Richard deposited the key. He had already settled his bill and had taken the compliments from reception and thanked them for their help.

Peter pushed the luggage into the car, Richard climbed in and they made their way out of the apartment drive for the last time. Peter switched the air conditioner on, the evening air was oppressively humid and the car needed cooling down.

'Thanks, Pete.'

'No problem. We thought you might like to just have a meal at home, so Sheila has made Spaghetti Bolognese, you okay with that?'

'Sound's great.'

'And tomorrow you shall sample my culinary skills when I cook Souvla, I will do some of the preparation tonight; and you can help if you like.'

'Yes, love too; you really are becoming a local, aren't you?'

'I suppose so, but it's that kind of place, everyone who likes it settles in and gets used to the way of life. We have, but I know some people who couldn't hack it. Spent six months then went back to England, couldn't get away fast enough.'

'That's sad and fancy trying it only for six months.'

'I know, but that's it; I think you either become a part of it or you don't, there's no middle ground. I know some people and places who try to keep themselves separate, but over here you really do have to integrate, otherwise you miss out on a lot.'

'Pete, I think you being a part of Goddess Dives is good for all of us involved in this.'

'It's kind of you to think of me like that.'

'I have to tell you, Pete, all my working life I've trying to find the thing that would 'Make Me'; I suppose everyone does; but few actually manage it, do they?'

'I suppose that's true.' Peter spun the wheel and took the Pissouri turning.

'The thing is that now I do have that possibility of making it happen. But I'm scared, really scared that I can't handle it.'

'That's strange, Rich, why do you feel like that? It's your baby. You had the belief all the way through; after all it was you who found her.'

'And I wouldn't have if it hadn't been for you.' Richard owed what he had to Peter.

'Well, that's just my luck that I was the one to help you.'

In that short conversation from Limassol, they had outlined their plans, aspirations, fears, and worries; it was a healthy way to start a business.

After the evening meal, Peter took out a large bowl of meat; chicken and pork which he started to marinate by throwing some olive oil and spices over it and then mixing it all in. Sheila sat on a kitchen chair and drank cold white wine. The men chatted as Richard decided to get his hands dirty; he kneaded and mixed the cold meat which now glistened and his fingers became pungent with the scent of garlic. Peter placed the dish in the fridge to let it settle in its juices overnight.

They sat down to watch a programme on TV. Peter had a four-metre satellite dish out back so he was able to pick up most programmes, including Sky and BBC, they decided on an episode of East Enders.

Richard was not a soap fan, but it was a reminder of home and how much he missed his wife. 'I'm going to unpack, and then ring Julie.'

Sheila got up and showed him his room. 'You're through here. Do you want anything, coffee, tea, brandy, me?'

Her last remark took him by surprise, was it a joke or meant as a come on? 'No thanks, Sheila, I'm fine. I'll just get settled and then probably come for a coffee.'

'Good. And you go ahead and make yourself at home, ok?' Sheila smiled a covertly wicked smile as she opened the door and Richard placed his suitcase and bags inside the room.

He started unpacking; hanging some clothes in the wardrobe, placing smaller items into the drawers, and positioned Aphrodite's figurine on the bedside table. Then he placed the alarm clock next to her; it was a subliminal thought, that this was what he was getting up for every morning.

Julie answered after three rings. 'Hi, how are you?'

'Busy. Another batch of letters came for you yesterday and I can't get through them fast enough. They all want to talk to you about a deal or an idea or some sponsorship, or some advertising, it just doesn't stop and there's a documentary on tonight on Channel Four about Aphrodite and your discovery. It doesn't let up, Rich; it's incredible, what about you?'

'It's the same here; people just keep coming and coming. We had two coaches of Japanese waiting at the site before we opened this morning. But the press seems to have gone a bit quiet, not so many news crews now. Oh, I spoke to Peter and made him a partner, sixty/forty. So now we have to set up a company and make it all legal.'

'That's really good, I think he's a genuine asset as you say, and they're nice people too.'

'How are Molly and Matthew?'

'Molly is still away, and so is Matthew. She says she'll come out with me again once things settle down.'

'Great, that's great. You know, we could start her off in an English college over here if she wanted too, before she sets off on her gap year.'

'Maybe; but we'll see. Because first, we have to see how much this business makes. It might be good now but give it some time, see if it will really make us a fortune, don't you think?'

'Yes, you're right. But as Peter keeps pointing out we're not in high season yet, so fingers crossed it will take off. Oh, Jules, we have changed things around a bit. Pete came up with a new design for the ropes and we have more people able to use them now.'

'See, I told you he was a good asset.'

'Tomorrow we are having a barbecue so I will talk to them in more detail; I just wish you were here with me.'

'Well, it's going to take a while now. I haven't even begun to sort out the house, what with all these offers coming in, but I will get around to it this week. Then I'll send you emails of the best offers so you guys can mull over them.'

'Thanks, there was something...' He wanted to tell her about the figure on the beach, but something else told him he shouldn't.

'What?'

'Just I love you.' It was a copout.

'I love you too. Take it easy in that sun love and be careful, eh. And don't go talking to any strange women.'

'No, not likely, I am far too busy for that. Ok, speak to you tomorrow, Bye.' The cell clicked dead and he lay back on the bed, content that things were going well both at home and out here.

Peter knocked on the door of his room. 'Hey, Rich, there's a documentary on Channel Four about Aphrodite, want to watch it?'

'Sure, coming.' It would seem that Peter could get Channel Four as well.

The fire was lit in the fugo—the metal box Richard had seen so many times during his visits to the old town of Limassol. However, today he saw it in action as it held the three rotating spikes over the white-hot charcoal. The smell was aromatic as the oregano and spices cooked and flavoured the meat as it slowly churned, browned, and sizzled succulently in the intense heat of the fire. Souvla was the traditional way of cooking meat, and Peter was as good as any local, the way he nurtured the meat and the fire, carefully looking over it to make sure it cooked to perfection, with the aroma so enticing and the flavour mouth-watering.

'Nearly done' Peter enthused as he sat drinking a cold beer whilst the meat turned. 'Another beer?'

'No thanks, Pete, this is just fine.'

Sheila came out onto the patio with a large bowl of salad and some dips: Taramalosalata, Dhashi, Hummus, and a large carton of Yoghurt, as well as black and green olives.

'Can I do anything?' Richard looked around at them both, waiting to help.

'You can bring some Pitas, thanks.' Pete was already beginning to take the skewers off the fire and placed the meat in a Pyrex bowl.

Richard collected a handful of Pita-bread, placed them on a plate and took it to Peter, who positioned a silver-coloured lattice tray over the coals. The pitas started to cook and brown almost instantly as he turned them over after twenty seconds one side, and then the other. When done, he dropped them into the small wicker basket that sat next to him and placed that on the tray with the Pyrex bowl. Everything ready, Sheila mixed the salad and Richard placed the hot dishes on the table, the dips perfectly positioned to make dipping easy.

Peter poured some wine into their glasses and offered a toast. 'To Goddess Dives.'

'Goddess Dives.' they all joined in the toast.

'Let's eat.' Peter announced.

The order was acted upon without hesitation as forks and spoons first then plates were filled. It was evidently clear that Peter was a good cook and the proof was on the first bite of the pork, it was succulent and delicious and the gusto with which everyone ate was either because they were hungry or the food tasted so good that it would be criminal to waste.

'Pete, I think we need to set up a company as soon as possible. Do you know someone who can do it?' Richard finished chewing his last piece of chicken as he offered the question.

'Yes, I can ask Larry, he's a financial adviser out here, and we use him on the bases. I'm sure he can do something. He does offshore too, and that's why so many companies use Cyprus for their business, they avoid the tax that way or at least pay a lot less.'

'Good, well, if you can fix it so we can meet with Larry.'

'He's away in the UK at the moment but will be back soon enough. I'll call him and set it up.'

'Oh, and I'm going to make Julie and Sheila also shareholders, that way they have some voting rights as well.'

'Really? Thank you, Richard. It's all very exciting, isn't it?' Sheila had a beaming smile on her face and a little trace of hummus. She was obviously pleased with the suggestion. 'Richard, I wanted to ask you something... it is a bit personal and you don't have to tell me if you don't want to.'

'What is it, Sheila?'

'Then you don't mind telling me?'

'What is it?'

'Come on, love, spit it out, Richard said he will answer you.'

'How much have you taken so far, Richard?' It was a question that perhaps was more than a bit pertinent in light of their present conversation and Peter too was curious.

'As of yesterday, it's nine thousand Euros.'

'How much?' Even Peter seemed shocked.

'Good god.' Sheila's face turned a whiter shade, as if in utter shock. 'And it's...'

The two men joined in together. 'Not even high season yet.'

The laughter that spilled out across the terrace was infectious and in that moment the three of them realised that they could indeed be on their way to a fortune.

'This calls for Champagne.' Peter rose from his chair and made his way to the fridge.

Sheila edged her seat closer to Richard. She looked at him then studied him closely, focusing on his eyes, looking for any kind of signal that her flirting was welcome.

Peter appeared oblivious to Sheila's moves and presented the bottle with three glasses before popping the cork and the liquid flowed liberally. It was the cue for more celebrating and the beginning of Goddess Dives Limited.

CHAPTER SEVENTEEN

BEAUTY ON THE BEACH

The first two days of the week were fantastic, people came in their hundreds and the way all involved handled them was like a military operation. The customers moved so smoothly up and down the ropes that they could easy process one hundred people every half hour; and the money just kept on mounting up. The top road was full of cars that had parked on the side and for the first time since the launch, there were also a number of boats offshore, small craft that nestled on the waves just waiting and watching.

Two days flew by and during that time Richard did not see the mysterious woman again. He was even beginning to think he had imagined it. His mind was well occupied with lots of other things anyway; yesterday he had gone through several emails that had come from Julie and tonight Peter and he were going to chat about what would be the most interesting or lucrative. Things were going well, but first he had decided to meet with Costa.

He had over the past two weeks got to know Costa better and they had enjoyed many a good coffee and chat together. But now, Costa wanted to talk business, so Richard agreed to meet with him after the site closed, arranged with Peter to close up, and he would go see the man.

'I'm off to Costa, you okay to lock up.?

'Yes, fine, no problem.' Peter was already out in the water making his way to the ropes.

'Do you want to come?'

'No thanks, Rich, you take care of it. Besides, I just want to get out of this and get in the shower.' He held his vest up, sniffed under one armpit, and his expression gave the right signal that he was stinking.

Richard laughed and began walking up the shingle beach towards the steps, but as he got closer, he spotted a girl. She lay on the beach at the water's edge, her body so close to the waves that it looked like as if she had just been washed ashore. There was no one else close to her. Even at that distance he knew it was the same girl from before although her hair looked different. There was a braided ring that covered her forehead like a laurel leaf crown. Her legs were long, slender, and the same golden brown tone as the rest of her body. She lay motionless, embracing the sun.

Richard approached carefully, so as not to startle her, in fact, almost stalking to make certain she didn't move. He was five feet from her when her legs started to dance in the air, moving in harmony as she waved them effortlessly back and forth, the warm breeze catching her light brown tresses and her loose costume, which was a light golden colour and practically flesh tone in texture. He could see her body through it, the perfectly formed breasts that were hidden from sight by the flimsiest of fabrics, the hint of a nipple underneath and the long luscious legs that he followed with such attention to the middle of her body.

'SHIT,' He spoke so loud he was sure she heard him. Of all the times, he had left his camera behind, but if he went to get it, he knew she would be gone by the time he returned. He got as close as he could without drawing further attention to himself, although clearly, he must have, just by hovering so close to this beauty on the beach. He was mesmerised, speechless, and yet at the same time so very anxious to talk to her. But why? What was it about her that made him so desperate to first find her and then talk to her? He summoned the courage and drew a little closer.

She turned and faced him.

Her eyes pierced his, holding him transfixed. And neither did they blink, or move, keeping him unbalanced, not knowing which way to look. Enchanted, he moved forward and tried to speak in his best guide-book Greek. 'Yassoo Tikanis.'

It was a pretty reasonable stab at communicating, but she didn't react she just kept looking at him. It was a look that implied previous knowledge of him.

'Emais, Richard, isis?' It was a request for a word, any word.

She said nothing simply adjusted her body, and offered another glimpse of her immaculate figure. Saying with one gesture that she was fully aware of her powers of manipulation to entice and tantalize not just Richard, but any man. Slowly, she stood up. She was almost as tall as Richard, statuesque, proud, and beautiful.

Faced with her looking directly at him, Richard blurted and spluttered in English, like an excited child. 'I've seen you before. You were here... just a few days ago, I saw you then and tried to talk with you but you were gone when I tried to find you.'

Without acknowledging anything he had said, she began to move away.

He followed, still trying to make contact. 'Where are you from?' He was so eager to hear her speak; he kept firing questions. 'What's your name, where are you from?'

She stopped and pointed to the sea.

'The sea... Thalassa? Is that where you're from? Who are you really?' Richard fired.

She turned to him, lifted a hand, and stroked his face.

It was a soft touch, a lover's touch, a loving touch; there was magic in her fingers. He could feel his entire body shake and shudder. He had never been touched like that before, never experienced so much feeling. Her fingers had barely brushed his skin but he felt as if he had been given a new soul, her eyes kissing his.

'You know who I am, Richard, you brought me here. You brought me back. And when it is time, I will come for you.' Her language was a mix of Greek and English yet it was poetic in its delivery, a voice that spoke melodiously, with gentleness and promise of a new beginning.

It was the last sentence that Richard couldn't take in. He sank to the sand in front of her, his senses confused and infused. He shut his eyes for a moment and when he opened them again she was gone. He looked around in desperation, scouring the ground in front and behind him, but she was nowhere.

'Mr. Richard, what is it, Mr. Richard?'

Costa came hurrying towards Richard as he saw bewilderment on his face and sheer panic in his eyes.

The sun was almost down now, where the time had gone Richard had no idea.

'Mr. Richard. Are you okay?'

'Did you see her?' Richard begged for some sort of confirmation for what he had seen and experienced. He held out his arms to Costa, as if he were trying to catch some invisible thing.

'See who, they have all left, there is no one here. Please, come with me, we have a drink now. A strong one, yes? We go now away from here.' Costa held Richard's shoulder and steered him off the beach and up the steps.

As they climbed the stairs, out of sight of them and everyone else, the beauty on the beach sat astride the rock, looking down on the shore below, just as the sun set on her.

CHAPTER EIGHTEEN

CATWALK TO THE MOON

Over the next week, Richard could not get the image of the girl from his mind. It was like an itch that he couldn't reach; irritating, yet when he thought of her it eased the irritation. It was like a trigger in his mind, and it clicked in when and wherever he was. She just kept popping into his head and there was nothing he could do about it. He tried to distract himself with thoughts of home, Julie, and the children, or of the work he was trying to do but those very thoughts took him back here, to the rocks, and to the girl, and he would be back where he started, trying not to think about her. It was catch 22 and he was in the middle of it. Slowly but surely, he was losing his mind.

He had relied heavily on Peter during that time and on Wednesday complained of being feverish and taken the day off. But even when he tried to get away from the rocks, everything reminded him of her. He saw her face all over, in the streets, the bars of Limassol, or on the road sitting in a car, everywhere he looked he saw her. Could he be so utterly obsessed, or was she genuinely tormenting him? And if so, why? What had he done? Had he read the signals wrong? Did the Goddess not want to be found? After all, she had lain in those waters for 5,000 years. Perhaps he should let her lie there for another 5,000 or more. But how could he have got it so wrong? He convinced himself that he had not, that she really wanted to be found, and then it clicked. Did he honestly believe that the girl on the beach was real, that she was the Goddess come back to life?

Subconscious recognition woke him up and dragged him back to reality, like a heavy thump on the back of the neck. In that one sentence he had shaken himself from his stupor of fantasy and woken up in the real world. Tomorrow, he would go back to the rocks and forget all about the Goddess and mystery women, he would concentrate on the cash in hand, and that was certainly adding up.

He spent the evening with Peter and Sheila discussing some of the plans and proposals they had been offered. One of them was an Aphrodite Water Slide based at the rocks. Both the graphics and design looked impressive, and it would probably turn into a real crowd pleaser. But that would require handling by the Paphos authorities. Richard could not do anything about that but it was possible he could help set it up.

The other offers were mainly for merchandising, and there were some smart and colourful designs to consider and undeniably a cut above the ordinary tourist trap stuff. They could also brand their name on the designs as Goddess Dives, which was also appealing. They sat, drank, chatted, and made their plans then walked the short distance back to the house. Peter and Sheila said their goodnights and Richard opened his bedroom door. He would sleep better tonight, of that he was sure, because tomorrow was a new start at the rock.

The tide lapped against the rocks, as small groups of white crested white horses out at sea gathered ready to parade on a one-way ticket to the shore. They swept over the blue ocean and bathed it in bubbles and fizz, as several of the white horse waves gathered in mass and height, some rising above the others to form larger waves of pure white spray that boiled and frothed with every movement; two of these split from the rest and cascaded towards each other, rushing together into a delicious mix of foam and sea and through this conception, a woman emerged pure and clean, gliding out of pure energy then walked out of the sea. Dolphins escorted the woman as she edged her way through the waves to emerge perfect, her figure clothed in a flimsy white slip that was transparent against the moonlight.

This was the image and the classic pose that Ursula Andress had encapsulated as she arose out of the sea and into movie history. The sea grew calm as it gave up its prize. As the woman walked serenely to shore, her hair caught by the night breeze, her body was a picture of beauty and lust personified; sleek, feline, sensual, and sexual, all things in one; and it was this image that became the miracle. For she was not just one woman as she walked ashore, she became all women; as her body changed from one iconic image to the next, from Cleopatra, to Juliet, to Helen of Troy, to Marilyn Monroe, and from child, to wife, to mother and grandmother; created in her image. As a finale to her show, she turned and walked back to the sea. A single beam of moonlight shone down, creating a line that stretched far out to sea and the horizon in the distance; she paused and waited for the waves to subside then climbed on the beam and took her first steps down the catwalk to the moon. As Aphrodite moved down the beam, an ominous figure emerged from the darkness, dressed all in black.

Richard shuddered as he watched the woman arrayed in the cloak of night follow his goddess, only to disappear into the moonlight.

Aphrodite's last words to him echoed across the waves as darkness returned to the shore. 'Soon, Richard, soon.'

Richard woke from his dream; she was back in his head.

CHAPTER NINETEEN

THE POSSESSIVE SPIRIT

Richard's fall from reality to insanity was becoming more difficult for him to disguise and both Peter and Sheila had noticed subtle changes. At first, it was the way his mind would suddenly switch off in conversation; as if someone had stepped into the room; but then came the pronounced mood swings, where he would suddenly get up, leave the room, and not come back for an hour or two. Or he would wait behind after working at the rock and not get home until almost midnight. Where he went and what he did they never asked, but the frequency of the night outings had increased each week. They also realised that doubtless they might have to intervene soon, but for the moment they felt it was best that he worked things out for himself.

Richard no longer spoke to Julie as often as before, their conversations were becoming stilted, and his emotions were no longer as strong as they had been when she had left. In fact, he was becoming resentful that she had gone back; he even started blaming her for the way he felt. But when he spoke to her he kept those emotions hidden; tried to play the everything-is-normal card and for a while it worked.

Julie had not been married all these years without knowing that something was afoot, something didn't read right, or ring true. Whether it was in his voice or just the way he spoke, her intuition told her that she needed to get herself out to him and quick because the conversations they were having meant only one thing, Richard was having an affair.

But given that her suspicions were not proven, she could not simply drop everything and return to Cyprus; she needed to convince herself at least fifty percent that there was more than a chance she was right. She waited until next morning when Richard was at the rocks before she called Sheila. But before she did, the phone rang.

It was Sheila. 'Hello, Julie. Yes, fine, thanks. How are things going? Is the house rented yet? No, we are all fine here, and Richard seems good since he moved in. Yes, maybe a bit tired. No... Good, really great, the business is just so busy. They can't believe it, I don't believe it. So when do you think you'll be coming over? No, No problems. I just think Richard's missing you, that's all... oh good. Really, another week then, yes... Ok Julie, bye for now.' Sheila hung up. 'Maybe it will be too late by then.' She spoke softly to herself.

At the other end, Julie thought the same thing, but for different reasons.

The second week of June saw the temperature rise sharply, it was now well into the 70's and the clock hadn't yet got to nine am. Peter was ferrying people along the ropes but Richard was once again pre-occupied, looking about the place for his elusive mystery woman. The last few days had seen him deteriorate noticeably. It was beginning to show in his features, his well-tanned face displayed tell-tale worry lines that had broken out across his eyes and mouth, his hair had begun to recede faster, and he had lost weight, a lot of weight. In just a few days, his normally muscular frame had become frail, slowly but surely his energy was being sucked out of him.

Peter had tried to talk to him but when he did, Richard ignored him. Peter's affection for his friend was slowly eroding, as their relationship diminished with each passing hour. Peter was carrying the business now; Richard was a passenger, and the change was also noticed by Marcus and his companions, who also showed their concern for Richard's sudden fall. But none of this stopped the people from coming; it was something that Peter couldn't fathom. What was so special about a few rocks in the water, no matter what they represented?

As if seeking proof, Peter called out to Richard at the other end of the rope. 'Look at this crowd. After a month, they still keep coming; more and more each day. Richard, Richard! Richard!

'What?' Richard's one word answer was confirmation enough that he wasn't listening.

'It's like these people have come for baptism or something... don't you think? Ducking the head in water; very symbolic.'

'Hmm, yes'

'Did you hear me, Richard? I said… oh fuck it, just forget it.'

Richard continued to scan the faces in the crowd and on the beach.

Peter's frustration was becoming forceful as he swore and pointed and it grew even more tangible as Richard suddenly dropped the rope and walked off down the beach. He shouted and screamed after him; 'Richard! Richard!'

Richard scoured the shore and the crowd searching for his secretive woman. He ran up the rocks and stretched his neck to see over the top of the crowds, but there was no one who looked remotely like her. His obsession for her and passion were intense. He wanted her badly and had to have her because he had finally discovered a love he never dreamed existed within him.

Julie had only ever been the love of his life and he had experienced all the emotions he thought possible with her, but with the Goddess it was different. She was inside him, inside his mind, inside his soul, and inside his body. What she felt he felt, what she craved, he craved, the desire, the emotion, the very essence of life that she had breathed again was now his breath. As she breathed so did he. Together they were keeping each other alive. This was what she meant by 'you brought me back'. But to do it he had to sacrifice his own life, or the life that he knew to do it.

The Goddess or 'The Mistress of the Rock' was indeed a possessive spirit. But he knew his reward would be her; that alone was worth the sacrifice. But as hard as he tried, he couldn't find her. As he wandered aimlessly, ahead of him, in a rocky outcrop, he saw her... he ran from the rocks across the hot sand and stones. He fell once but got up again and continued running. People stopped what they were doing and stood watching as this man came hurtling past them, his face bathed in sweat, with a haunted look etched across it.

Richard could see her; she lay on the rocks, her body soaking the sun rays. The waves were barely a few feet from her as they crashed against the small rocks, without splashing her. With trembling hands, he clambered over the rocks towards her. In the process, he cut his hand on a sharp edge, which made him wince and the hand bleed.

The girl did not see him approach until he was almost on top of her. Not recognizing him, she screamed loudly, a piercing scream that alerted others nearby and they came running to her aid.

Richard stood still. She was not the one. He didn't speak, just bowed his head almost in shame and skulked back across the rocks, leaving the girl shaking and upset.

Two guys tried to chase after him but he ran faster and faster away from them and they gave up the pursuit after a few hundred yards.

It was too hot to run. Richard moved slowly through the crowd and sat, taking deep breaths, trying to get his body back into working order. If it was possible on a crowded beach full of people to be alone, then Richard had achieved it.

CHAPTER TWENTY

YOU ARE LOSING IT

Arriving at the house, Richard said nothing, and just went to sit in his room. He lay on the bed staring at the ceiling for a while then he picked up the book next to the bedside table and began to read.

Peter arrived an hour or so later. He was hot, angry, and his face soaked in sweat. He banged on Richard's door. 'Richard! Richard!' He hit the door again.

Richard opened it slightly; his timidity was clear as he stood looking at Peter and Sheila, who had joined her husband.

'What the fuck is going on, Richard? Where were you all afternoon? I had to run the place on my own, where the fuck were you?'

Sheila tried to calm her husband. 'Please, Peter, your language.'

'Fuck my language, Sheila. I want to know what the hell is going on. What the hell is wrong with you, Richard? Just look at yourself.'

Richard held the book in his hands and gripped it tightly. 'Nothing, nothing is going on, I just felt tired and I had a headache, that's all.'

'A headache, who the hell are you trying to kid here? You fucked off and left me. So, where were you?'

Richard scuffled away from the door. 'I didn't go anywhere.'

'I don't believe you, who were you with?'

'No one, I was with no one. Well, no one that you know.'

'What! What the hell does that mean, you were with someone then?'

'No, I wasn't, she wasn't there. I couldn't find her.' Richard moved closer to the bed as the door swung open.

'Who are you talking about? Not your mystery woman?'

Sheila looked at her husband. 'Mystery woman?' she asked.

'Yes, he keeps seeing some mysterious woman on the beach, who is never there when I look. Ostensibly, she just appears to him.'

'She is there, she has always been there.'

'Who?' Then, as if a light bulb switched on in his head, Peter sat down on the side of the bed.

Richard backed away.

'You're not telling me that the woman, your mystery woman, is the fucking goddess, are you? Not the Bitch from the rocks. Are you really trying to tell me that, eh, Richard, are you?'

'Yes.' Richard's one word was greeted with silence.

Then, Peter began to laugh,

Sheila smiled a nervous smile, she didn't like this, she did not like this one bit.

'Richard, get a grip, will you, you're losing it.'

Richard stood and looked straight at Peter. 'You want her for yourself.'

'What did you say?'

'She said this would happen. Said it would be like this, first the doubt, then the envy then the desire and the betrayal. She said it would be like this. But I found her, she's mine. Stay away from her.'

'You do, don't you? You really think that the woman you have seen is the Goddess.'

'She is.' Richard insisted.

'It's laughable, Richard, if it wasn't so pathetic!'

'You can think what you like but I brought her back and now she's coming for me. She promised me.'

Sheila moved forward to hold Richard. 'Please, Richard, please think of Julie and what this could do to her and the family. Think of them instead of any other woman, real or Goddess.'

'Yes, Richard, listen to Sheila, and think of what you have.'

'Please, get a grip.' Sheila was almost begging him.

Peter moved closer to Richard. 'Yes, you found her, that much is true, but she's a pile of rocks, under the sea, and that's all she is. You've let yourself become possessed by her and her myth.'

'She is real and I'll prove it to you. I will prove it to all of them.' Richard's defiance was commendable but unwarranted. He sank to his knees.

Peter looked at the sad figure of a man he had grown to respect and admire and now detested, he shut the bedroom door and left Richard to wallow in the self-pity that he alone had created.

'You must call Julie, Sheila; she has to know what's going on.' Peter's anger had soothed.

'Yes, I will. She said she was coming out next week, but I think she should come sooner.'

'The sooner the better. I saw something like this in the forces, it's a sort of aftershock; it crept up on one of the mates I knew without warning and within a few months he had lost his mind.'

'You think this could happen to Richard?'

'I think it has already started.'

'Then we have to keep him away from those rocks; he can't go there again because I'm afraid of what he might do.'

'He won't do anything. But if you come with me tomorrow, we will keep him here, lock the door if need be. But we do have to keep him away from the rocks.'

Sheila began to realise how quickly her plan was taking shape, and the odd thing was that it was happening on its own. She did not need to manipulate anything, as poor Richard was spinning his own web into which he would fall in and be trapped. But for the time being though, she would keep those thoughts to herself and go along with Peter as the dutiful wife.

Richard heard the clock as it ticked loudly on the bedside table, he heard the insects outside as they chirped, chattered, and clattered incessantly into the evening. The noise of a stray dog barking in the distance, echoed across the streets, the sound of a car door shutting joined the ensemble. He wiped his hand across his face, the moisture had stopped and his mouth felt dry. He climbed off the bed, stood facing the mirror above the sink, and peered into the glass. The gaunt tormented figure that stood looking back at him showed just how far he had fallen, his face had aged, and he had grown five perhaps ten years older in a few weeks. He lifted his shirt; before it was a snug fit, now it flapped about his body, his muscle wastage pronounced. He turned on the tap and the hot water ran into the bowl. He washed his face, removing the dirt and grime. If only he could wash away the hurt he had caused just as easily, but he knew that wasn't possible. Tomorrow he would need to find a new place to live.

Richard sat in his room silently, ignoring the tray of food Sheila had placed before him. He had no appetite, had taken just a few sips of the cold water, and sat back on the bed. He attempted to clear his mind, but no matter what he tried to think of she kept coming back to torment his senses. When he shut his eyes, he saw her, when he covered his ears he heard her, and when he thought of nothing else, she stood naked before him taunting and teasing him. It was exquisite the way she possessed him, never allowing a free thought, always controlling and manipulating him to her will, just by promising herself. But exhaustion finally pushed him into sleep. It was a place he did not want to visit, for he knew that even there she moulded him to her desires and wishes. He loved her, and he hated her.

The darkness was something he could touch, a thick heaviness that he pushed through like a black fog; which enveloped him, the more steps he took. It swirled around him, moving him backwards and forwards. He held out his hands in front of him but couldn't see them; there was nothing there except gloom; then he felt something.

It felt like a cold vapour which drifted across him like the breath of a ghost. He tried to move forward but his path was blocked. He stepped aside and reached out. A hand clasped his; it felt wet and clammy, as it gripped and held him, dragging him through the fog, and into the light.

There, he could see clearly where he was; on the beach at Petra Tou Romiou. Ahead of him was a table, laid out in all its splendour, full to overflowing with fruits, meats, poultry, and a large suckling pig that took centre stage as its body steamed from its recent cooking heat. Richard watched as the first guests took their seats and a bevy of beautiful scantily clad Grecian women danced along the table as the Gods of Olympus joined the party. He recognised the figures instantly, Zeus, Poseidon, and Ares from their costumes, but their faces were the people he knew, Zeus was Lukas, Poseidon Costa, Peter Ares, and Sheila took her place beside Zeus as Hera.

He moved closer and wondered why they couldn't see him; even though he was standing a few feet from them. Aphrodite entered, carrying before her a large golden platter. It sparkled and shimmered and the guests applauded as she placed this large golden dish gently on the table. She turned and beckoned for Richard to go to her. They all turned their gaze to him.

'R I C H A R D,' There was no mistaking that voice anymore.

Richard found that his legs could now move again and he took a few tentative steps towards the table. The eyes of the Gods were upon him as he drew closer. Aphrodite urged him to come closer, and edging forward, he stood beside her. She passed her hand over his face, as she had done at the beach and the same sensations ran though him just as he had felt then. She held his hand and together they placed their hands on the golden dish. They lifted the lid. On the plate lay

Julie's head. Richard screamed and screamed and Aphrodite's maniacal laughter ripped through his dream and into his mind.

Peter slammed the door open and grabbed Richard. He could feel his heart near bursting; his body was dripping and his eyes rolled in his head. 'Get a doctor, Sheila, get a doctor now.'

'No, no Doctor, I just need sleep. I had a bad dream, that's all. Please, no Doctor.' Richard begged, trying to keep the incident private.

Peter saw the hurt in his friend's eyes and relented, and took pity on him. 'All right we won't get a Doctor, this time, but if this happens again, then I will.''

'Yes,' Richard agreed. 'But it won't, I promise. I just need to sleep. Just let me sleep.'

'Okay, but you stay here tomorrow and rest. Sheila and I will take care of things and Sunday the site is closed, so you will have the weekend to recover.'

'All right, I'll stay.' A sort of calm began to sweep through Richard. He felt his body relax as if the grip that held his mind suddenly let go. His eyes didn't feel so heavy;

Sheila passed him a glass of water. She had crushed a sedative into the water to make sure he would at least sleep through the night.

He drank it down and laid his head back on the pillow.

Peter threw a sheet over him and then switched off the light.

Richard closed his eyes and for the first time in days, he saw nothing.

Sheila was already on the phone. 'Yes Julie, I think you should try to get here soon. Yes, it's Richard. He's in a bad way… and we can't really explain it. We think you need to come take care of him… Can you move your ticket forward to tomorrow? No, he's sleeping now… we don't know, Julie, we don't know what it is; I just think that you need to be with him. Let us know what plane you're on and Peter will meet you… He's okay for now but we won't tell him you're coming… just see when you can get here… call me back, okay? Bye.'

Julie called the number on the ticket wallet and explained that she needed to get to Cyprus urgently; the flights were full until Saturday night, when there was a plane at 22:30, which would arrive at Paphos about three am. It would have to do.

'I will be there about three am and I can get a taxi. It will save Peter coming for me.' Julie's voice shook.

Sheila could hear the anxiety in Julie's voice but she also wanted her to have some sleep tonight. 'No, it's fine. Peter will meet you between three and four. It will be that late by the time you get through customs. Take care and see you tomorrow.'

It was perhaps the shortest telephone call there had been between them but it was also the most important. Because once Julie was back with her husband, things would sort themselves out. Sheila prayed that they would, as it looked like as if her own plans were starting to come together. With Richard out of the way, she could bring them to fruition.

CHAPTER TWENTY-ONE

DELIVERANCE

Peter had risen early, for two reasons, first he needed to check on Richard and second, he needed to make sure that Sheila had breakfast. He cooked her scrambled eggs on toast and made her a pot of hot tea. Working in that heat no matter how well covered with sun block, creams, or lotions, you needed covering inside too. A healthy breakfast would make sure that Sheila had all things covered.

She appreciated the gesture and kissed her husband lightly on his lips in gratitude. She too had to make sure that she was adequately covered which was why she chose to wear her especially fashioned one piece. It was slightly longer than a normal costume, as it covered almost three quarters of her legs and arms, the ultimate in sun protection. And together with her large floppy sun hat, that concealed most of her head and face, she felt ready for what lay ahead.

Peter sported his NY baseball cap, a souvenir from a trip to the Big Apple and one of the new *Aphrodite Rock's* T Shirts. He also wore long Bermuda shorts, bright red in colour so he could be seen in the water easily. If things didn't improve with Richard soon he might have to take over running the business permanently or at least until Richard's return.

Richard was asleep, the shutters tightly closed, no light seeping in, just a soft beam shone on the floor through the open door as both Peter and Sheila checked on him one last time. Once they shut it, Richard would be back in the dark. Peter closed the door and the two of them made their way outside to the car. Sheila climbed in and Peter started the engine, it revved twice then it moved off the driveway and into the road.

Richard waited for the car to leave then climbed out of bed and dressed quickly, not bothering to shave or shower. He just needed to get the sleep out of his eyes and the taste of the night out of his mouth. He drank a glass of orange juice and searched for his keys. They weren't in their usual place hanging up by the door. He opened drawers and cupboards searching for them. Had they taken them? Panic was returning, and with it visions of the Goddess. His mind had not been disturbed for eight hours by her face, now she was back. He opened more cupboards and drawers then pushed open Peter and Sheila's bedroom door and threw their stuff to the floor in his continuing search for the keys. He went outside to the garden, just opening boxes and throwing pots around. He had to find them. Where were they?

Alarmed, he ran to the car, and found the keys still in the ignition. Leaving the house with the front door open, he started the engine. He drove fast and furious off the driveway and almost hit a car as it screeched to a halt beside him. The driver swore in a barrage of Greek words which he ignored as he pulled away from the house and into the road. The mark left by his tires evidence of the speed he was moving at. He flashed into the road and past two cars then gunned the engine, pushing the car to its limits as his foot thumped down hard on the accelerator. He hammered the gears and crunched them, he couldn't drive fast enough. And all the while the words were in his head repeating over and over.

'Come to me, Richard, come to me now.'

He pushed the car as hard as he could, its guts being ripped apart as he drove with venom along the road and made the turning on almost two wheels as he rounded the corner to Petra Tou Romiou. The road ahead was full of traffic. Slamming the brakes full on, he slid the car to a halt. He jumped out of the car, while hearing her voice calling to him.

'Come to me, Richard, come to me now.'

He slid down the rocks and onto the shore.

Peter and Sheila had split their customers into groups, which were moving in an orderly and efficient way. The atmosphere was light and fun and the people were happy. That was until they saw the maniac running across the shore towards them.

Peter moved quickly but not quickly enough as Richard stormed into the water, while pushing several people under as he crashed past them, their bodies upturning as he thrashed through the waves to the rocks.

Peter struggled after him and the people milling around the ropes watched in panic as the man kept smashing the waves with his hands. He looked as if he was trying to claw the water, and some children burst into tears as they stared at the bewitched and helpless man smashing his limbs against the water, the waves washing against him and pulling him under.

'She's here, she's here. Where are you, where are you?' He screamed, his voice becoming louder with every shriek then felt the tears run down his face as Peter grabbed and held him tight.

Peter was soon joined by Marcus and two of the others. They dragged Richard out of the water and laid him down on the shore. His whole body was shaking.

'Oh my God, Peter, what has happened to him?' Sheila stood looking down on the shattered figure of their friend.

'We will close the site now, please, everyone, just go home. Signomi, ella... please go home.'

The people began to drift away, their day ruined, with only a sorry memory to take home as a souvenir.

'We have to get him out of here, to a doctor or a hospital. He can't go on like this; the damn place is draining him. Look at him, Sheila, just look at him, he's dying, this place is killing him.' Peter said as he held Richard's arms.

The spirit that possessed him so completely in the water had subsided. He was limp, without feeling and his body felt relaxed as they picked him up and together carried him to Peter's car.

Sheila followed behind and took Richard's keys from him. 'It's Saturday, the hospitals will not see him until Monday, unless it's an emergency.' She pointed out as she knew all about the local hospitals' rules of engagement.

'Okay, I'll drive him back home then. But call the Doctor, and maybe he'll be there by the time we arrive.'

Richard sat back in the chair. He didn't move or resist, just sat smiling, a knowing smile, a secret smile that only he had the answer to.

Peter looked at him. How he would love to know what was in his mind right now. What had taken place that so changed his friend into the husk of the man who sat in the passenger seat beside him? He began the drive back to the house.

Sheila followed in Richards's car. She had left a message for the Doctor to call her and thankfully, her cell phone rang within three minutes of the call. She explained that their guest had had a sort of attack or seizure, so could he come quickly? The Doctor gave a response of forty minutes; it wasn't great but it would have to do. Sheila's audible response to herself was. 'They take less time to deliver a Pizza.'

Julie had cleared everything she needed to and ordered the cab to pick her up. She had told the children that Dad wasn't well and she was going to pick him up and bring him back home until he got better. She wasn't sure how long she would be but they would both be back as soon as was possible.

Molly offered to go along but Julie insisted that she would be better on her own and that she should rather stay to keep an eye on the house. Matthew too promised to return home and be with Molly, so that front was clear; it left her free to concentrate on the most important thing, namely, bringing her husband home.

Peter opened the car door to pull Richard out. The front door was wide open. He carried Richard inside then dumped him onto the sofa before he checked the rooms; they looked ransacked. Drawers and cupboards thrown on the floor with clothes and linen scattered all over the beds, but nothing appeared to be missing.

Richard lay back on the sofa.

Sheila pulled into the driveway, climbed out and walked into the chaos. Her pristine house now spoilt and flawed. 'What the fuck happened here?' She stood staring at the mess. She was upset and angry simultaneously. 'Peter?'

'I'm not sure but it looks like he was searching for something and left the door open when he found it, but thankfully, nothing seems missing. It's just a mess, that's all. It's okay, I'll change the locks. Now let's get him into bed. What time is the Doctor coming?'

'In about ten to fifteen minutes. He said he would take forty, and that was twenty-five minutes ago'

'Here, Sheila, just take hold of his hands and arms and let me carry him.' With Sheila's help, Peter hoisted Richard onto his shoulders, fireman lift style, and carried him down the corridor, into his bedroom, and let him flop back onto the bed.

Richard had not moved since being brought in and still had the same smile on his face that he had when he had first been shoved onto the passenger's seat.

As Peter stood looking at him, it reminded him of the 'One Flew over the Cuckoo's Nest' movie where Jack Nicholson finally lost his battle with sanity. Was this the same truth now for Richard?

The knock on the door interrupted Peter's harrowing thoughts and Sheila ushered the Doctor in. He took one look at Richard and began to administer to him. Peter shut the door and left the Doctor to his trade.

'Peter, what are we going to tell Julie?'

'We won't have to, she will see for herself.'

'She won't have left yet, should I call her and tell her what happened today?'

'No, don't do that. Let's not give the poor woman any more worries than she already has. Christ, she is probably worried sick. And she will know and see soon enough for herself... I am going to have a large whisky, you going to join me?'

'Yes, make mine a double.'

'I thought you didn't like whiskey.'

'Today is an exception, just pour it, please.'

Peter poured two double whiskies, neat, the nearest thing to medicine they had. They drank them slowly without a word being said.

The Doctor came out of the bedroom and stood before the two of them. Peter offered him a whiskey and then a seat.

He declined the whiskey, but sat down. The Doctor was a small man with broad shoulders, probably in his late forties or early fifties; he wore a dark blue shirt and tie, grey trousers and brown shoes, the comfortable shoes variety, as he often did a lot of walking. He spoke English with just a hint of a Greek accent, which probably meant that he had been schooled and educated in England, but still retained his Cypriot roots. He also wore a pair of rimmed glasses that did not sit neatly on his nose. 'Your friend is very ill. He is suffering from a form of Catatonic Schizophrenia, and he experiences hallucinations which are dangerous to him. He was the one who found the body in the rocks at Petra Tou Romiou, yes?'

The two nodded.

'I think he has somehow been affected by the environment there, maybe the sun or the water possibly. This happens to people with this condition, they see and hear things, and it is not surprising as Petra Tou Romiou is a very strange place, and some people say it is bewitched. Your friend has become one of these who have fallen under its spell. But, perhaps it is not so strange, especially when you are dealing with a place that is so steeped in history and myth, because the mind can play tricks. I believe Mr. Cole has become so wrapped up in Petra Tou Romiou that it has taken him over. He is also hiding something... I am not sure what that is, but he has it in his mind it must be a repressed memory, buried deep in his subconscious. Do you know if he ever experienced anything like an accident or a death in the family?'

Peter was about to say something but Sheila glared at him, so he said nothing. Unwittingly, he had just been inducted into Sheila's plan.

'No Doctor, not that I know of... can we do anything for him?' Sheila baited the question.

'Immediately, he needs rest, then he needs to get away from the rocks if possible, he should leave the island. Every moment he spends here, it just reminds him of and draws him to the place. Back home in England, running to the rocks will not be so easy. I am sorry but that is the best medicine I can give him. I have however given him a shot so he will sleep for ten to twelve hours, he won't get up again.'

'His wife is arriving tonight; we are going to collect her.' Sheila offered the sentence as a way of saying they were doing their part.

'That is good. Once she is here, it will take his mind off the rocks and then she will need to get him home quickly.' The Doctor stood and shook hands with Peter and Sheila.

'How much do we owe you, Doctor?'

'Nothing, your friend has done a lot for this island and it has cost him dear. It is a pity that it has come to this but there is always a price to pay for new-found fame and riches. Yassas.'

Peter showed the Doctor to the door and shook his hand once more.

'Please take care.'

Peter felt that those words were meant for him and not just Richard.

Sheila sat on the arm-chair with a contented look about her. She sipped the whiskey slowly and her thoughts began to whirl in her head. *Catatonic Schizophrenia, hmm... doesn't sound good that. It sounds perfect.*

Peter came back into the room, his mind on Richard and the Doctor's prognosis. Picking up the whiskey, he too sipped the ice-cold liquid slowly. He stood and looked straight at Sheila as if wanting to tell her something important. 'Richard had problems in the Gulf. He was on a particular reconnaissance mission... well, more like an observation one... and he never got over what he saw.' He put down his glass and went across to the table to collect his laptop. He plugged it in and as soon as it started, he Googled Highway 80 and clicked on it. 'Sheila, come and look at these. Do you remember right at the end of the Gulf War there was an attack on HIGHWAY 80? Look, here are some of the pictures...'

Sheila looked at the images in disgust. 'They are horrible, just horrific, put it away.'

Peter closes the laptop. 'Yeah, and Richard told me there was a woman dressed all in black who blew herself up in front of him, took out a US Corporal and her baby…' Peter paused as he recalled the conversation the two had had in the tent.' 'He had terrible nightmares about that… so I think that's the memory the Doctor is alluding to. He has Post Traumatic Stress, that's the polite expression for it Soldiers Madness is more like it.'

'The poor lamb.' Sheila's sarcasm was almost plausible as she churned possibilities and opportunities over in her mind. 'Well, it's a good job that Julie is coming for him. And once they've gone we can start some plans of our own.'

'What do you mean exactly?' Peter looked straight at Sheila; he could see the wheels turning in her head as she spoke.

'It's obvious, my love.'

The term of endearment felt strange in Peter's ears.

'Poor Richard, can't do this anymore, so we take over and talk to Mr. Christo whatever his name is, and tell him that we are in charge. No, you are in charge, and will operate the site and of course split the money with him as pre-arranged. It will be our little nest egg and just to show you how much I appreciate you, I have a little surprise for you.' Sheila moved closer to him and ran her hand up his thigh. 'Do you want to have your surprise?' She took his hand and led him into their bedroom. To make sure he got the message. This was the sacrifice she needed to make to ensure he understood what she wanted; she just hoped it would be over quickly.

In the three hours since the Doctor had left, both Sheila and Peter had looked in on Richard at least four times. His door was becoming a revolving door, but each time the result was the same. He was out of it, the shot working like a dream, though what dreams he was having remained his.

Peter sat drinking another whiskey, Sheila read a book and both feared that if they switched on the TV the news would be broadcasting the events of the day. They did not want to know what others were saying, just wanted to forget about it, at least for a few hours. The press and media would soon be all over them, they were sure of that, only this time, it would be their turn for the spotlight.

Julie sat nervously in her seat on the plane. She hated flying at the best of times but usually any flying she did was always with someone she knew, either the kids or Richard. This was the first time in years she had flown on her own, except of course when she had returned home just a couple of weeks ago. The young woman next to her seemed too engrossed with her earphones and her magazine to want to indulge in conversation, or anything that would take Julie's mind off the flight. The in-flight movie came on; she switched her attention to the screen and waited for the title. Mr. Bean's Holiday flashed up on the screen. 'Oh fuck, not Mr. Bean.' She heard herself complain, but sat back in her seat to watch it anyway.

Sheila and Peter had fallen asleep on the sofa, the day's events had exhausted them and neither was as young as they used to be.

Richard slept.

Julie also slept, the movie had made her shut her eyes and she had managed to doze off. The night crept slowly forward.

All was still at Petra Tou Romiou, the waves making the only sound as they swept in and out across the shore, the moonlight cast a beam through the centre of the two rocks, and a warm breeze drifted over the stones. Two lovers stood looking at each other, in the most romantic place on earth.

CHAPTER TWENTY-TWO

WHAT HAPPENS NOW?

Julie waited at the carousel musing. She had not expected to return so soon and how quickly things had changed since the last time she had stood here and was about to again. The clerk at the desk in the UK had promised that she would give her bag priority clearance, and sure enough hers was the second off the plane. She grabbed it, dumped it on the trolley, and headed for the exit. The plane had been delayed by forty minutes, so it was just after 4:30 am when she pushed the trolley through the exit door and into the arrivals hall.

Peter left Sheila at home, who began preparing for Julie's arrival. Again, she made checks on Richard. Fast asleep. Now alone in the house, she moved back into their bedroom and opened her wardrobe. She began looking through her clothes, found a long black piece of material, draped it over her shoulders then pulled it up over her head. She smiled, liking the dark reflection.

Peter hugged Julie, a little tighter than they had done when they met. This was more like greeting a relative not seen for a long time.

The hug was enough to tell Julie that something serious was happening.

'Good flight, was it?' Peter's non-descript comment meant nothing, merely a way to break the awkward silence.

'How bad is he, Peter?'

'We are not sure, The Doctor saw him today, and said he thinks he had some seizure.'

'How is that possible? He's a fit man, who hasn't even had a cold in years.'

'It's not physical, Julie, it's his mind. The doctor says it has something to do with the rocks, the place has somehow affected Richard.'

'What, how is that possible? He was so excited about finding it and making it work and in the space of four weeks he has lost it, how can that be?'

Peter opened the boot of the car, pushed Julie's bag inside and opened the door for her, just as the first glimpses of sunlight began to appear like a thin line across the night sky. He started the car and they moved off out of the car park. 'Julie, I don't know how to tell you this.'

'What is it, Peter? But I think I know anyway.'

'What do you think you know?'

'I have suspected it for a few days now.'

'What, Julie?'

'Richard has found a woman, he's having an affair and the guilt has affected him.'

'No, Julie, that's not it. Well, at least I don't think it is. If it was it would be easier to explain.'

'What do you mean?'

'Richard believes... and this is not easy to say without you thinking that I have gone crazy too.'

'For Christ's sake, Peter, tell me, I need to know.'

'Richard believes that the Goddess is alive, that he brought her back, and she is coming for him.'

'You're serious, aren't you?'

'I am. Only today he ran into the water and thrashed around looking for her. He terrified the people so much we had to close the place. He disturbed everyone.'

'Oh my God! He really believes this, doesn't he?'

'Yes, Julie, he does.'

The car turned off the road at Pissouri and entered the narrow streets. As it approached the house, the first signs of a new dawn were breaking through.

Sheila, who had been waiting at the window for their return, opened the front door. No one was sleeping much this night. Sheila, like Peter, hugged Julie and planted a kiss on her cheek. She almost had tears in her eyes.

It was clear to Julie that they had gone through something, which they would have preferred not to. 'Where is he, Sheila?'

'He's sleeping. We put him in the bedroom at the end of the corridor, the last door, if you want to go and check on him, but maybe you should wait until he wakes.'

'No, Sheila, I want to go and see him now.'

'Of course,' Peter moved Julie's bag into the hall and she stepped over it.

She walked quickly along the stone floor and into Richard's bedroom. He was still sleeping, but she could see even in those first few seconds how much he had changed. He had lost weight and his face was, although heavily tanned, thin and drawn. His hair had receded and his forehead was now clean of hair. He moved once, turning on his side. Julie slipped off her shoes and lay next to him.

She didn't cuddle him or cradle him as she wished she could, she just lay next to him and watched him breathe.

Peter and Sheila waited for a few minutes for Julie to return, she didn't.

Sheila was the first one up, she had tried to sleep but it had not been easy. Peter on the other hand managed to continue his slumber even as she drank her second cup of coffee.

The morning had already passed by the time Julie came out of the bedroom and entered the kitchen. Richard was stirring and she thought it might be better if she was out of the room when he woke up. Who knew, he might have another attack if he saw her lying next to him.

Sheila poured a large black coffee for Julie, although she had not slept for long, the events unfolding had made her wide wake.

'What do you know, Sheila, when did this start?'

'Honestly, I don't know. When Richard came here he was fine. He hadn't had any sightings then, or at least he didn't mention it. This really started about two weeks ago when he and Peter were at the rocks and Richard said he saw someone, a beautiful girl.'

'She would be, wouldn't she?' Julie's sarcasm was on the button.

'Well, at that point Richard kept going off, looking for this mysterious woman, then at night he would suddenly get up and leave the room and not come back for a couple of hours, or he would stop behind after work and not come home till midnight.'

'And you didn't think this was suspicious?'

'Julie, what are we going to say? He's a grown man, it's not our business to ask what he's doing or where he's going. We were curious, even worried, but as long as he came home and didn't stay out all night we didn't think we could say anything.'

'Yes, okay, you're probably right... Sorry! Go on, please.'

'Then a couple of days ago, it happened again, only this time, there was an incident on the beach. A girl accused a man of stalking her. People said it was Richard, but there was no proof.'

'Oh my God!' Julie was shocked and surprised, especially as she knew her husband's character well.

'Peter tried to find him, and when he got back he lost it. He accused Peter of wanting the woman for himself, and then it all came tumbling out that Richard's woman was the goddess of the rocks. At first, it was funny, and then it became very sad and very dangerous.'

Peter came into the kitchen and joined his wife; having overheard much of the conversation. 'We decided that Richard should stay here the next day and gave him a sedative to keep him calm and help him sleep.' Peter continued. 'But he got up and stormed out of the house, leaving it in a mess... I think he was looking for the keys. I was stupid and left them in the ignition, so he was able to drive to the rocks. It was when he got there that all hell broke loose, he was like a man possessed. He crashed into the water, knocking over people and then started smashing his hands against the waves and screaming. 'Where are you?' Just kept yelling at the top of his voice.'

Julie's expression could not match the fear she felt inside her. She was finding it hard to fight back the tears, not just for herself but for her husband.

'We dragged him out of the water and brought him here, Sheila called the doctor and he diagnosed Catatonic Schizophrenia.'

'No, this can't be... it's just too bizarre. What happens now?' Julie's plea was heard but no-one was sure what to say to her.

Sheila offered her hand and clasped Julie's, 'You have to get him out of here, and take him home, and quick. Peter, will you check the flight schedules, see when they can fly back? Tonight, if possible.' Sheila motioned to her husband to call.

'No problem, I'll do it now.'

Julie stood then walked to the lounge, looking out at the street from the window. 'Is it possible for someone to become so fixated with a place that they believe what they see and hear is real?'

'That is what the Doctor thinks,' said Sheila.

'I don't understand any of this.' Julie began to cry, the emotions that had been swelling now bursting forth as she sobbed repeatedly.

Sheila held her tight and stroked her head gently, soothing the troubled woman as tears rolled down her face, doing her best to console her.

Peter left them alone and went to make the phone call from the kitchen, speaking softly so as not to wake Richard down the passage. Returning, Peter felt embarrassed to interrupt and spoke apologetically. 'Excuse me, Julie,'

'Go ahead, Peter.'

'There are no flights until tomorrow midday. I've booked two seats and requested a last-minute cancellation should one occur.'

Julie nodded her appreciation and slipped away from Sheila's embrace then glanced at the clock. It was 7:45am.

Sheila and Julie sat in the armchairs; both had drifted off to sleep, missed lunch, and now both were hungry. Peter made pasta and salad in the kitchen whilst they chatted.

'Peter has a theory about all of this.' Sheila was trying everything she could think of to rationalise the situation.

'What is it?' Julie was curious to hear it.

'He thinks Richard is going through a Cult Crisis, like those people who become sect members and do the will of those who command them, even down to committing suicide.'

'Richard, a cult member? I don't think so.'

'Ok maybe not a cult member, but a sort of follower, and in this case a single member, of the Cult of Aphrodite.'

'Really, that's an interesting hypothesis.'

Sheila continued with her explanation. 'In ancient times the site did have a cult following. There was even talk of human sacrifices there—most of that was legend—but they have found evidence of cult rituals and things.'

'And how is Richard involved?' Julie questioned Sheila for more answers.

'Well, not directly, just that he shows signs of being a cult follower; his single mindedness and jealousy are all elements of this behaviour.'

'Perhaps, but I think it's the sun that has affected him. All that heat, sweat, salt, awful conditions to work in, and in the water for eight hours a day... and all that pressure as well, it can't be easy. I'm sure I would go mad too.'

Sheila could see Julie didn't want to believe it and was in denial. 'Yes, maybe, but as soon as you get him home, he will be safe and away from that place and all that it stands for.'

'What about the site, we had better get in touch with Mr. Lukas and tell him what has happened, I am sure he will want to close it down for a while.'

Julie's words surprised Peter and Sheila equally. Neither had considered the possibility of Mr. Lukas discontinuing the daily ritual.

Sheila snatched at her chance to make her claim. 'No need to worry there, Peter has already spoken to Mr. Lukas and he has asked Peter to continue just until Richard gets better. We didn't say too much, but he must have heard about Richard's rant at the beach. So Peter called him.'

Peter now complicit in Sheila's lie said nothing as Julie stood staring out the window.

'Good, thank you, Peter. At least that is something off Richard's mind. The less he has to worry about the better. You are a good friend.'

Peter brushed off the compliment; the guilt he now carried was his alone. He disappeared into the kitchen and began to prepare a tray of food which he carried into the lounge. He placed the three plates on the table, sat down, and waited for Julie and Sheila to join him.

'Is there any for me?' Richard stood in the doorway, a weak smile across his face.

'Richard! Hi,' Julie rushed over and kissed him. Then hugged and smiled as she pulled back to look at him.

Smelling his breath and seeing his appearance, she was quick to comment. 'You need a shower and to brush your teeth, love.'

Richard could see she was there for him, even as she admonished him with his personal hygiene. 'Sorry I overslept, and sorry about everything.' He said looking at Peter and Sheila.

'Forget it, Rich, just go and get tidied up and come have something to eat.'

'I will. The sleep has done me good, I feel better now.'

'You go get yourself sorted, love, then we'll sit down and have a chat, okay?'

Richard turned and walked back to the bedroom.

Out of sight of her husband, Julie began to cry again, realising just how far Richard has fallen.

Sheila dropped a comforting arm over her shoulders.

'I don't understand any of this.'

'Before you judge him too harshly I think you need to see this.' Peter reached for his laptop.

Sheila remonstrated. 'Not while we're eating, afterwards.'

'Yes, sorry, after.'

'What is it, Peter? What do you want to show me?'

'I will after we eat.'

Richard seemed more relaxed as he made his way back to the bedroom. He had not expected to see Julie, expecting to ride this particular storm on his own but with her here it would be so much easier to go back and forget. Opening the door, a dim light from the open shutter caught something lying on the bed. Curious, he walked over. A shiny black cloth was spread out like a dress across the bed. He stopped, frozen, simply gaping at it. His mind ripped wide open as the noise of bombs, explosions, and screams tore through him and a long deafening scream reverberated in his mind. The terror had returned, the images unfurling carelessly again. He pushed his hands over his eyes and ears to shut out the light and sound from them, but a gentle whisper broke through.

'Soon, Richard, soon.'

He fell onto the bed and buried his face in the pillows.

With lunch over faster than intended, Julie prompted Peter to show her what he was going on about.

Sheila excused herself. 'I do not want to see this, so I'm going for a lie down.'

Now engrossed in the images, Peter and Julie ignored Sheila as she sloped away down the corridor.

'Did he ever show you these images?'

'No.'

'Maybe this will help you understand a little better.' Peter moved from one image to the next, each one more distressing than the last. 'And he was there!'

Her expression of utter shock, gave her a better understanding of Richard's pain.

Sheila crept silently down the corridor. Gently opening the door, she saw Richard had not bothered to clean up as expected, instead he was sprawled across the bed, his face burrowed deep in a pillow, and possibly fast asleep again. She bent over and retrieved the crumpled and discarded cloth from the floor then closed the door carefully behind her. A sly smile crept across her painted lips, knowing she had achieved what she sought. A couple more of those little pushes and her plan would be complete.

Richard's expected nightmare did not happen. He woke a little woozy but collected a bath towel, opened the bathroom door, and turned on the shower. The power jets hit the bath side and the room filled with steam. He climbed in and pulled the shower curtain across. He stood there a while, just letting the water cascade over him, washing not just his mind, but hopefully, also his sins. Gingerly, he soaped his body. The water was hot against his skin but he stood without moving for as long as he could then picked up the shampoo and lathered his head. The soap bubbles collected on his scalp and he rubbed them in, massaging his scalp with his fingers.

The visions had left him; he saw no faces or heard any voices. He let the water rinse the soap as it cascaded over him. Perhaps he was beginning to get his sanity back. He pulled the shower curtain aside and fought his way through the steam to the mirror. Written in the steamed-up glass of the mirror were two words.

TONIGHT, RICHARD.

Richard stood still, unable to move, his body frozen, in fear and exhilaration, now he knew for certain, she was coming for him tonight.

CHAPTER TWENTY-THREE

IT HAPPENS TONIGHT

Nobody said much as they sat at the table having their meal. Richard ate his food like an embarrassed child at a party, who had been especially naughty. Furtive glances across the table accompanied by nervous smiles was the way the rest were dealing with Richard's presence, and nobody seemed to want to ask anything.

Even Julie preferred to just eat and wait for someone else to speak. She knew once this icebreaker had happened that the words and questions would flow from her, but until that moment she would bide her time. The solution arrived provided by her own cell phone ringing in her bag, she excused herself from the table and went to answer it. 'Hello, Molly... No, we are fine. Yes, Dad's good, he's having his meal now with us now. Yes, he's fine. Do you want to talk to him?'

Richard held up his hand, 'no' he was not ready.

'Sorry, Molly, he's feeling a bit tired and he's gone to lie down. No love, he's fine, and we are coming home tomorrow. Give my love to Matthew, has he arrived yet? Oh good, that's good, yes, you have what you want, love, don't worry. Love you... Bye, bye.' Julie put the cell down and back into her bag.

Richard sat at the table staring straight ahead.

Julie went to sit down next to him. 'Richard, that was your daughter, who wants to know what is going on, and so do I.'

'I think I'll leave you two to have a chat. Come on Sheila, we're going for a walk.' Peter urged.

Sheila collected a short white jacket and draped it around her shoulders.

Richard sat opposite Julie and although they were a few inches apart from each other right now, miles separated them in other ways. She demanded answers but he switched off as she kept repeating the questions. He couldn't hear, he couldn't reply, all he could think about was the message on the mirror. 'Tonight, Richard.' It meant only one thing; he had to get out of the house by any means and down to the rocks.

'Richard, this is getting us nowhere, so when are you going to tell me about what has been going on here? Are you having an affair? I just need to know... What is this bullshit about the rock and the Goddess? What is that about? I told you I would not share you with anyone, flesh or fantasy, so are you fucking some other woman and using this madness to cover up your guilt, is that it?' Julie's American accent was more pronounced than it had been in months.

The last comment hurt Richard. Of course, he was not having an affair, but naturally, all the signs looked as if he were. The incredulity of the Goddess coming to life was also too much of a fantasy. So he was stuck, between a lie and a legend. If he confessed to an affair, Julie would divorce him, but if he confessed to an obsession, he could end up in the mental asylum. He had only to wait a few more hours and he would have his answer, but in the meantime, he had to buy time. 'I'm sorry, Jules, but you are right, I am having an affair.'

Her slap hit hard and hurt but her tears hurt even more as she slammed the door and walked out the front to catch her breath. She stood out there silently for a very long minute before she pushed the door open and entered the room again. 'Who is she, Richard?'

'No one special,'

His bland reply was even more hurtful, because in her eyes, he had sacrificed his wife, his home, and his children for no one special. That was so much worse than if he had said she had been the best-looking woman on the planet. 'Peter has two seats for us to go back tomorrow.' She announced. 'You can stay or come back with me, and if you do, I want you out of the house by next week. Collect your things and get out, is that understood?'

Richard nodded; he never expected this reaction. He wanted to tell her he was lying but the truth was harder to comprehend than the falsehood.

'I will sleep out here tonight. Tomorrow we'll fly home and then you can start putting your things together as soon as we're back in that house. Do you understand me?'

Julie's statement demonstrated just how much his confession had smashed their relationship because it was all in pieces. Richard turned silently away and walked back to his bedroom. His plan had worked, but what a price he had paid!

Peter and Sheila returned to find a distraught Julie. Weeping in a chair, she had not a trace of make-up left, the constant wiping of her eyes, face, and cheeks had cleaned her face of all traces and left her looking pale and sickly.

Sheila held her close and cradled her.

Peter poured yet another round of whiskey and handed a glass to Julie.

She sank it and coughed. She hated whiskey. 'He is having an affair. He told me.'

'No... I don't believe it.' Sheila argued.

'Call it a wife's intuition, but the bastard confessed. And with no one special, he said.'

'That's terrible, just terrible, the bastard.' Richard was now a bastard in both women's eyes.

Peter said nothing and just drank his whiskey silently.

Richard lay on his bed staring at the ceiling and then his watch. It was almost seven o'clock; the afternoon had flown by, the evening would soon follow, and then it would be time.

Peter and Sheila prepared a late supper of sandwiches and coffee, nothing too elaborate.

Julie sat in the armchair, and she had picked up a book and was doing her best trying to read it.

Peter moved to collect a tray and put a plate on it.

'What are you doing?' Sheila was quick to react.

'I thought I would get Richard something to eat too?'

'You stay right there, he is not having another thing from this house. Leave him there and don't you go and give him anything.'

Peter knew when it was best not to argue with Sheila and this was one of those times. He put the tray back, sat on one of the kitchen's chairs, and picked up the newspaper. The headline read, 'President set to honour rock's finder.' If only he had taken them around in the car instead of the helicopter.

The house was quiet; it had just turned eleven fifteen. Richard's door squeezed open. He had switched the light off, careful not to give himself away, then stared at the stone floor corridor, that would be difficult enough to get through without being discovered. Taking his shoes off, he tiptoed as quietly as he could to the lounge. Julie was sleeping on the sofa-bed. Carefully, he made his way into the kitchen and deftly collected a set of keys without making the slightest noise. His watch showed seventeen minutes past eleven.

Creeping slowly and noiselessly, he left through the backdoor. The outside light kicked in, he opened the car door, started the engine, and reversed quickly out into the road.

Sheila heard the faint noise first, got up, and looked outside the window, just in time to see a car moving up the road. She put her dressing gown on, walked into the bathroom, looked in the mirror, and saw the word 'tonight' faint on the glass as the hot steam rose from the tap. She switched on the lights and called out. 'Julie, quick, come here.'

Julie woke from her nervy sleep and rushed to see what the commotion was about.

'Look, Julie, look.' The word was clear in the steam.

'What's the time, Sheila?'

'It's about 11:30, why?'

'Oh God, no; Where's your car Sheila, where is it?'

'It's parked outside. Julie, what... where are you going? I'll get Peter.'

'No Sheila, there's no time, where are your keys?'

'They're on their hook. I'll get them for you.' Sheila ran into the kitchen. 'Damn it, they're not here.'

'What! Then where are Peter's? Get them, please.'

Peter was just turning over as Sheila switched on the light.

'Where are your keys?'

'What?' Peter asked sleepily, still in slumber-land.

'Your car keys, where are your fucking keys?' Then she saw hers, which she had forgotten on the dressing table. She grabbed them.

The last statement got Peter out of bed. Somewhat dazed and shaken by the two women flapping about in his bedroom, he pointed to his discarded trousers on the side of the laundry basket.

'Here.' Sheila threw her keys at Julie, and watched her dash from the house.

She started the car. It kicked over then stopped, and she started it again. The engine revved and then stalled. On the third time, she slammed her foot down on the accelerator and the engine roared. She hit the light switch and disappeared out of sight.

Still half–asleep, Peter realised it was the figure of a distraught Julie he had seen run from the room. 'What's going on, Sheila?'

She sat on the end of the bed and crossed her legs in a provocative stance, exposing her thighs, teasing him for that instant. 'You remember the doctor's visit, when he said

Richard was close to the edge.' She ran one hand over her nightdress, before she walked out.

Still stumbling from sleep to awake, he tried to listen to her mumbles as he searched for his clothes and threw them on. He followed her, putting his shoes on in the corridor and found her standing in the bathroom, staring at a faint word on the mirror. He leaned over, trying to see more clearly. 'You were saying something about Richard and the edge...' He stopped and stared at her reflection.

'I just gave him a little push!'

Peter stepped closer to the mirror. 'That is your writing. What have you done?'

'I just gave him a date with his Goddess.'

'What? You know how dangerous those waters are... There are no lights to see anything and the current is really strong. Now do you know what you have done?'

'Looking after number one, Peter! Think about it, he has made so much money in such a short time and with him out-of-the-way it falls to us to keep it going. Without you, he would never have done it anyway, so he owes you. This last episode should just about put him, as I say, over the edge. You should thank me.' Sheila revealed the black fabric she had been holding behind her back.

'You calculating absolute bitch. I knew you were conniving but this is...' He raised his hand, as if he meant to slap her.

Sheila was afraid for a second, because she cowered and covered her face from the blow, but it never came. Instead, he pushed past her and turned to scream at her, his anger at a level she had never witnessed.

'And just so you know and don't you delude yourself, I know all about your cosy lover George or Georgiou, or whatever his fucking name is. So here's the thing, what you wished on Richard you shall get. When I get back I want you out of here. You can piss off to Georgiou and whatever wonders he has to offer. You understand me.' Peter slammed the bathroom door shut and ran to the hall, took his car keys, and slammed the front door behind him. Getting into the vehicle, the engine started right away and he screeched off and away from the driveway.

The house was still and quiet as Sheila walked back to Richard's bedroom, contemplating her actions, and honestly, she was not sorry either. Why did everyone else get the breaks, where were hers? Resting her head on the pillow, she noticed Aphrodite's figurine. She picked it up and kissed it before hurling it against the wall, where it shattered into a thousand pieces.

CHAPTER TWENTY-FOUR

DESTINY

Richard was still thinking about his false confession to Julie. He had never really lied to her in all their married life, at least not on this scale. There had been the odd white lie but never anything as serious as this, and he hated the idea that if things went wrong tonight the last thing she would take from him was a lie. But as he drove to the site, he felt a new energy entering and infusing him, as if he were shedding the skin of normality and becoming someone special.

Thankfully, the road had light traffic as he drove along which meant that it wouldn't take him long to get there. He glanced at his watch and then at the dashboard clock; they were synchronised at 11:35pm. If it was tonight, it would be midnight.

Richard eased through the gears as he rounded the bend into Petra Tou Romiou. Costa had packed up; there were no lights on at the restaurant. He parked the car in its usual place, opened the car door, walked across to the steps, and then down them quickly. His body had found new vigour, the languid feelings had gone, and he felt better and stronger, which he might need to draw from for what lay ahead. As he moved over the stones towards the rocks, he saw the six metal spikes in the water sticking out; he drew closer to the edge and to the waves that slipped up the shore. He checked his watch, 11:50. He would give it another five minutes.

Slowly, he removed his shirt and threw it to the ground then pulled down his shorts and kicked off his sandals. Smoothing his hair with his fingers, he noticed for the first time how much it had receded. He moved closer to the water and felt its icy lick across his feet and in-between his toes. Naked and alone, he walked into the waves. The first one hit him as his body acted like a breaker, the second took his breath away for a second, and the third hit him full on.

It was becoming colder with every wave, as the water also crept slowly up his body. Close to the first rock, he let his body glide into the watery mass then stretched out his arms and began to swim; his head and face dipping in and out as he moved slowly out to the furthest rock. In his mind, he kept repeating over and over, 'Three times around the rocks and you find your true love on the third time.'

His body beat hard against the waves as the current began to take control and he swam faster and harder, beating back the pressure from the current as he tried to fight against the formidable force then he heard her voice.

'It's time, Richard, it is time.'

He thrashed in the waves, his strength returning as he fought hard to complete the first circle. The second lap made him stronger as he knew that with every stroke his destiny was only one more lap away. He slapped the water harder with his arms, a wide smile spread over his face. He was close now, so very close; one more turn and he would see her for real. No more pretences, no more dreams; he would finally see her and once he did, he would be with his goddess for all time. He pushed himself to go one more time but the waves were taking him down.

Of course, this was a trial, he sensed it. She had to test his resolve to see what he was willing to do for her. For a moment, the reality of an unfounded tribulation upset him, because had he not given up enough for her already, had he not sacrificed everything he had? Nevertheless, he kept swimming, even as he felt his chest being crushed against the lapping waves, the pain becoming harder to bear as he gasped for breath. But he was almost there; just half another turn and it would complete the last lap.

As he turned for the last time, he lifted his head and saw her. She lay on the waves, her body glistening in the moonlight, her breasts exposed as if to taunt him further with the promise of things to come... She called to him, a soft chant that made him push himself beyond endurance. His destiny was just ten strokes away. He lifted his head again and opened his eyes.

'Richard! Richard!'

Odd, but that voice did not belong to the Goddess. That was Julie's voice. He turned his head and saw her in the water by the third rock. She had somehow swum out from the other side and was now before him, bobbing in the water, her face just barely visible as the waves beat across and into her.

'Your one true love, Richard, your one true love.'

The words hit home like a thunderbolt; all this time he had sought his 'one true love' and the reality was that he already had her.

Julie was struggling and he battled through the waves. As he did, the current grew stronger and Julie started going down. But it was not through a natural occurrence, he could see the hand pushing Julie's head down; the hand of a woman not of this world was holding her under. Richard wrestled not only the elements but his own body, if this was the last thing he did, he had to save the woman he loved. As he reached them he pushed Aphrodite away.

The siren-like scream ripped through the night air and caused Richard to let go. As he grabbed Julie from the Goddess, she sank below the waters. 'No, Richard, it's me you want, you want me.'

But the Goddess' pleas met with no reaction, Richard was too busy diving below the water to reach for the drowning Julie. He gripped one arm and pulled her to the surface. The waves below them began to foam and bubble then twisted, starting small flowing whirlpools designed to suck them in. Richard fought against the waves and surfaced, while holding his wife tightly and hoped against hope that they would be able to reach the shore.

The Goddess began to beat the waves with her fists; she too would not give up without a fight.

Almost at the shore, his strength was ripped from him as he fought for breath. Julie's weight weighed him down through the waves and the sharp rocks below started cutting into his feet as he staggered blindly in the now growing darkness. The full moon had all but disappeared as clouds sat neatly covering it in a misty blanket. Richard was mere feet from the shore when he heard the rumble behind him, which began below the surface and echoed loudly.

It was a deep threatening rumble that ricocheted off the rocks beneath the water and sent them flying high into the air, like a volcanic eruption. The stone shrapnel cut through the night, splintering and sending shards of sharp rock onto the beach. The metal spears rose from invisible slots and hurtled towards shore. Richard held Julie close to him for a second then let her go so they could dive underwater to escape the spears as they crashed against the rocks and around them. The pyrotechnics grew louder and more violent as rocks and stones flew like shells towards them but surfacing, they huddled for protection behind a large rock. Julie's naked body clung to Richard's naked body, and the embrace was one of survival and pure love for each other.

Enraged, Aphrodite continued turning her wrath against them, as she summoned the heavens and the winds to hail and rain down upon the two mortals. The air seemed hot and cold simultaneously as the forces of nature and the gods met. Bolts of lightning—thrown with such force and power that only Zeus could have been the arm behind them—crashed into the rocks of Aphrodite, splitting the first one in two, and the second, which took the full impact of the crashing blow sank below the waters. Aphrodite held her arms upwards and the sky lit above her, a single brilliant white flash, so intense that to look at it would have cost someone their sight.

But this was Aphrodite's last act. As she began to sink, her body disappeared under the waves until finally she was gone. The seas quelled and the cove grew quiet as the two bodies crawled out from behind the rock that had kept them safe. They stood staring at the water as it ebbed and flowed, watching as the rock that had stood for five thousand years sank slowly into the sand and below the waters, its death slow and deliberate. The Mistress of the Rock had taken her own souvenir back with her.

Richard held his wife tight, as she buried her head in his chest and shut her eyes tight. He looked towards the direction of the sinking rocks. On the shore the woman of his nightmares stood staring back towards him, she kept her eyes focused on him then turned away to walk into the sea. Richard watched as the waves swept in and covered her, he looked again, she was gone. The clamp that he felt around his heart, became loose and he could breathe properly again.

He cradled his wife towards him. 'Jules, are you okay, are you all right?'

Julie, stunned, shaken, and shivering looked up at her husband. 'She was here, she really was here.'

'Yes, she was! But how did you know what to do?'

'You're not the only one who reads guidebooks.' His wife smiled back at him.

Holding her in a tight grip in his arms, he tried to cover her with his body. 'They will have to rewrite them now.' his words would soon reverberate around the island.

Peter came running down the steps and threw a blanket over Julie's naked body and offered Richard his jacket. They watched as car headlights gathered above them to floodlight the stone battlefield.

Peter's look was one of bewilderment, he could think of only one thing to say. 'Is it over?'

Richard's stretched across and took his hand. 'It's over.'

CHAPTER TWENTY-FIVE

THE END

Sheila was not in the room when they got back to the house in the morning and Peter gave the impression that she was still sleeping as he gathered their bags to take outside to the car. On the drive to the airport no one said much at all, the road was relatively quiet. That is until they entered the airport road, where convoys of television crews and a posse of press and media people vehicles had gathered awaiting them. There were several hundred, or so it seemed.

'Stop here, Pete.' Richard said then he and Julie got out and made their way through the throng of anxious press and cameramen. He stopped and hugged his friend.

Julie kissed Peter as they became swallowed up by the crowd.

Peter got back in the car and drove away quickly, not in the mood for the insanity that was about to engulf them all. He did not even look around as Richard and Julie entered the departures terminal.

The posse of newsmen pounced on them as they entered the doors.

'Mr. Cole, can you tell us what happened last night?'

'Was it some sort of storm, Mr. Cole, what happened?'

'Did the Goddess appear to you, Mr. Cole?'

Richard said nothing, instead pushing the trolley over towards an official-looking man in the recognised dark blue uniform, as worn by police officers.

An obviously efficient man, he ushered them through, took their cases, and their passports then moved them to the check-in desk as the media waited. 'Mr. Cole, what happened?' The man asked and returned a pair of boarding passes. It would seem the authorities had their own agenda as far as the Coles were concerned.

'I will say one thing.' Richard addressed the waiting throng, flashbulbs intermittently hitting his face.

Julie stood beside him, looking proud and at ease in her husband's company.

'Have you heard of The Song of Bernadette?'

'Yes.' One of the newsmen shouted back at him. 'The film about The Lady of Lourdes.'

'Yes, the Lady of Lourdes.' Richard continued, 'At the beginning it says something like this. *For those who believe, no explanation is necessary, for those who don't believe, no explanation is possible.* Now we have to go.'

The bemused journalists and newsmen metaphorically were left scratching their heads, trying to sort out what to say as the TV reporters turned to camera.

Julie turned to him. 'I think you'll find it's for those who believe in God, no explanation is necessary, and for those who don't, no explanation is possible.'

Richard looked lovingly into his wife's eyes; 'Or should it be gods?'

Then hand in hand they passed through immigration and out of Cyprus.

The sheer number of people who stood looking down from the roadside onto the stone and rock littered beach at Petra Tou Romiou was too many to guess at. Everyone, it would seem, had converged on the place. Helicopters flew overhead, boats drifted out at sea, whilst the tractors below tried to gather in the shattered stones. The scene was one of total fascination and wonder. No one could give any answers as to what had happened. The only two people, who knew the truth, had already left the island. Speculation was rampant and the only thing on the lips of the people who stood staring from the road.

Across the road and from the multitude sat two men, who were drinking Greek coffee in the warm sunshine. The elder of the two was the unmistakable figure of Mr. Lukas. The younger man was not known. Lukas spoke to the young man.

'Well, that could have been handled better.'

'Yes sir. Do you think now that the rocks have gone it will be the end of this place?'

'No, it's just the beginning, my son, just the beginning. Her legend will live on for another thousand, maybe ten thousand years. Leave the box on the table when we leave.'

'Yes sir.'

Lukas finished his coffee and his water. 'I think we had better go now.' He stood up and placed some money on the table.

His companion placed a large wooden box down, just before the two of them left the restaurant.

Costa went outside and saw the box at the empty table. Walking over, took the piece of folded paper from the top and read the note.

Για το κοινοτικό ζ.   Which translated as, 'For the community, Z.'

Costa opened the box, it was filled with thousands of Euros; all the money that had come from the Aphrodite's Rock dives. Costa ran to the roadside to see the two men but they had vanished into the crowd.

Had he looked a little harder he would have seen the two of them walking away from the crowd and along the road. He may also have noticed the young man's sandaled feet and the two small wings that protruded from his ankles.

Below them, the feisty waves washed right up to the shore with nothing to bar their way to where once had stood Aphrodite's Rock.

THE END

Or is it?
The story continues in Scylla – The Revenge

About The Author

Born in 1952 in Orsett, Essex in England, the youngest son to Welsh parents Iris and Bill Edwards. Upon leaving school, he went into the travel industry, where he travelled the world, working in travel agencies, tour operators and airlines for some 30 years. In 1976 Myron began freelance writing for BBC, radio and television, his credits include The Two Ronnies, Week Ending, and The News Huddlines. In 1980, he joined JWT advertising, as a copywriter writing his first TV commercial for dog food inside 10 days. His love for the creative never left him and in 1987 he created Tubewalking, a new map concept, to help people get around London easier on foot, which still operates today. In 1990 he married Niki, whose family background is Greek Cypriot. On a family trip to Cyprus, visiting Aphrodite's Rock for the first time, the beginnings of his passion to write the story of Mistress of the Rock came into fruition. Moving his family in 2005 to Cyprus to live, gave him the opportunity to write, as during this time he worked on campaigns for TV and Radio in an advertising agency in Limassol. The first manuscript of the book was completed in 2007, released by a local publisher it had a limited audience, but was well received by those who had read it. He has now completed the sequel and is working on the third part of this story. Myron has three children, two sons and one daughter all grown up.

RockHill Publishing LLC

There are some lessons that only time can teach, but you do not learn talent, you only perfect it over time.

www.rockhillpublishing.com

CHECK OUT OUR OTHER TITLES:

ADULT FICTION:

Killer With A Heart

Killer With Three Heads

FANTASY:

Mistress of the Rock

The Emerald Lady

ROMANCE:

Knight Kisses

Love & Madness

When Dani Smiled

SCIENCE FICTION:

Pegasus: A Journey To New Eden

CPSIA information can be obtained
at www.ICGtesting.com
Printed in the USA
LVOW10s1432080717

540625LV00021B/109/P

9 781945 286148